A PROPOSAL
FROM THE
ITALIAN COUNT

A PROPOSAL
FROM THE
ITALIAN COUNT

BY

LUCY GORDON

MILLS & BOON

First published in Great Britain 2017
by Mills & Boon, an imprint of HarperCollins*Publishers*
1 London Bridge Street, London, SE1 9GF

Large Print edition 2018

© 2017 Lucy Gordon

ISBN: 978-0-263-07340-9

MIX
Paper from
responsible sources
FSC
www.fsc.org   FSC™ C007454

This book is produced from independently certified FSC™ paper to ensure responsible forest management. For more information visit www.harpercollins.co.uk/green.

Printed and bound in Great Britain
by CPI Group (UK) Ltd, Croydon, CR0 4YY

I dedicate this book to my Italian husband,
Roberto, who taught me so much about Italy,
and whose love inspired me
to set so many books there.

PROLOGUE

'I DID WRONG. I didn't mean to, but I couldn't help it. All in a moment I found that I could be wicked.'

The old man lying on his deathbed spoke weakly, for his strength was fading fast. Vittorio, the young man sitting beside him, grasped his hand and spoke urgently. 'Don't say such things, Papà. You're not wicked. You never could be.'

'Try saying that to George Benton. He was the man I robbed of a million, whose life I ruined, although he never knew it.'

Vittorio rubbed a frantic hand over his eyes and said fiercely, 'But that's impossible. How could he not have known?'

His father's eyes closed and he turned his head, as though too full of despair to say any more. Vittorio rose and went to the window, looking out onto the grounds. They were lavish, extensive, perfectly suited to the Counts of Martelli, their owners for five hundred years.

Franco, the present Count, lay still as his life slipped away. Vittorio knew that his father's mind had often been confused recently. And surely this was merely another example. Yet there was a desperation in the dying man's manner that warned him of something different; something fearful.

'Don't worry about it. Papà,' Vittorio urged, sitting by the bed again. 'It's all in the past.'

'It will never be in the past until it's put right,' the Count murmured. 'We were friends. We'd met here, in Italy, when he came on holiday. We became friends, and when I went to England a few weeks later I visited him. He was younger than me, and that made him fun to be with. We enjoyed a good time, going out for the evening, having a drink, charming women. And we placed a bet. It was just innocent fun—until his gamble paid off! He didn't know. He was too woozy with drink by then. So I cashed in his winnings, then supported him home and put him to bed.'

'What did you do then?' Vittorio asked quietly.

'I'd had the bank draft made out in my name. I did intend to cash it, and pass the money over to George once he was sober, but I fled before he could wake up.'

'And he never suspected?'

'How could he? I never told him about winning. The next day I cashed the draft and returned home to Italy. I never meant to do wrong. I'd just succeeded to the title, but my pleasure was tempered by the discovery of the debt hanging on the estate. Now suddenly I could clear the debt. The world was bright again. It was wonderful to have people showing me respect, calling me Count Martelli.' He managed a wry smile. 'Vittorio—my son—you'll soon know that feeling.'

'Don't, Papà,' Vittorio said with soft violence. 'I don't want you to die.'

The elderly Count squeezed his hand. 'You're a good son. But my time has come.'

'No,' Vittorio said fervently. 'You must stay with me a little longer.'

The thought of losing the father he loved was intolerable. His mother had died giving birth years ago. His father had raised him since then, and together they had been a team, each meaning more to the other than anyone else ever could. Now the man who was the centre of his life was

to be snatched from him, and the pain was ago-
nising.

'Fight it, Papà,' he pleaded. 'Another day, another month, another year. I'm not ready to do
without you.'

'You won't have to. I'll always be there with
you—in your mind, your heart, wherever you
choose.'

'I choose to keep you with me in *every* way,'
Vittorio whispered.

'My son—my son—there's just one thing I
would ask of you.'

'Whatever it is, I'll do it.'

'All these years I've got away with what I did,
and now that the end is near—' he shuddered '—I
must seize my last chance to make amends—with
your help. Promise me—swear.'

'I'll do anything I can. My word.'

'Find Benton. Ask his forgiveness. If he needs
money—'

'I'll give him whatever he needs. He'll forgive
you and you can rest in peace.'

'Peace? I can no longer remember how that
feels.'

'But you will have it, Papà. Wherever you are.
I promise.'

'Thank you—thank you.' Franco whispered the words over and over.

Vittorio rose quickly to pull the curtains across the window.

'Don't do that,' his father begged. 'You'll shut out the light.'

'I was afraid the sun was too dazzling for you.'

'It won't be for long.' He gave a sigh. 'Sunlight never lasts. You think it will. You think the light has come into your life for ever. But suddenly it's gone and there's only darkness.'

Vittorio sat down again, taking his father's hands in his. 'Darkness can be fought,' he said. 'I'm going to fight this for you.'

'One day you'll have your own darkness to fight. You can never tell when it will come, or what will cause it. You must always be ready for what you've never expected. Take care of yourself, my son. Take care—when I'm no longer with you…'

His voice faded.

'But you will always be with me. You must be. Can you hear me? Can you hear me Papà? *Papà!*'

But there was no response. Franco's eyes had finally closed and he lay still.

Vittorio dropped his head against his. 'I promise,' he whispered. 'I gave my word and I'll keep it. Wherever you are—hear me, believe me, and rest in peace.'

CHAPTER ONE

THE WORLD WAS full of light and glamour. Excitedly Jackie danced this way and that, rejoicing in the vision of her beautiful self that appeared in the mirror. Music played in the distance, inviting her into a universe in which she was the heroine.

But abruptly the dream ended. As she opened her eyes the real world fell back into place. The mirror's reflection showed not the luscious beauty of her fantasy but Jackie Benton, a slender young woman with a face that was intelligent, but not beautiful.

She sighed, easing herself out of bed.

Surrounding her was the austere bedroom where she spent every night. By now she had hoped to leave it behind, move to a new home and a more exciting life. But fate had arranged things differently, confining her to Benton's Market—the little shop where she lived and worked.

She'd spent most of her life in the tiny apartment over the shop that her father, George Benton, had started twenty years earlier. He had fought to make it a success, always struggling with money worries, and raising his daughter alone when his wife had left him.

In his last years Jackie had been forced to run the shop alone—something that had given her an unexpected satisfaction.

She was clever and hardworking, able to retain information about all the stock, and produce it at a moment's notice. Something which had at first impressed her father.

'You really remembered all that?' he would exclaim. 'Well done! You're in the right business.'

'I get it from you,' she had reminded him. 'I remember when I was a child there were lots of times you made people gulp at what you could remember without having to look it up.'

It had been a happy moment, uniting father and daughter. He had been proud—not only of her memory but her ability to choose the best stock. Knowing this, she had felt her confidence grow, and she had begun to see herself as a serious businesswoman.

Just occasionally her father had given her a little warning advice. Once, when a temporary employee had flounced out in a temper, he'd said, 'Did you have to be so hard on him?'

'I wasn't hard on him,' she'd protested. 'I just pointed out that he'd got something wrong. And he had.'

'You might have been a bit more tactful.'

'Oh, come on, Daddy,' she had said, in a teasing voice. 'What you mean is that a woman mustn't tell a man that he's wrong in case he's offended. But we're not living in the nineteenth century.'

He'd patted her hand. '*You* may not be, darling, but a lot of men are. You're a bit too fond of giving orders.'

'Too fond for a woman, you mean? You think I should just go along with him? Even when I know he's an idiot?'

They had laughed fondly together, but she'd come to understand that he had been making a fair point. She had learned to speak with more care, but it was still exasperating to have to do so when she knew she was an expert.

She had gradually come to enjoy the feeling of being in command—not merely of their employees but of the whole running of the place. She had chosen stock and it sold well. She'd had the instincts of a talented businesswoman, and they had given her hope for the future.

But her hard work had come too late. Matters had started getting worse, owing to the mountain of her father's debts that had piled so high that even her commercial success could not completely deal with it. Finally her father had been forced to sell the shop.

By then his life had been drawing to a close. Rik, the new owner, had reluctantly allowed them to stay in the little apartment upstairs, and Jackie had continued to work in the shop—but only part-time, so that she could always hurry upstairs to check that her father was all right. She nursed him gladly, giving him everything in her power in return for the loving care he had always shown her.

'It's so hard for you…to be caring for me and working downstairs as well,' he had said once. 'Such a burden.'

'Stop it, Dad. You could never be a burden to me. *Never.*'

'Bless you, darling. I wanted to leave the shop to you. I'd have been proud to give you a legacy. I hoped once— But there. It just didn't work out.'

She would have loved to own the shop. So

much of its success was due to *her* work, and it still held the atmosphere created by her beloved father. But she had known she must abandon that dream.

Her father had died a few days later. And then Rik had offered her a lifeline.

'You're welcome to stay if you become full-time. You can go on living here.'

She'd thought carefully before agreeing. She disliked Rik— an ill-tempered man in his forties—But she had accepted the job because it would give her a little time to work out her plan to escape into a new life—one in which she would have her own business, organising everything, using the talents she'd so gladly discovered.

Her dislike of Rik was well-founded. He had a high opinion of his own knowledge and skills, but Jackie felt that he actually knew very little. He made silly mistakes for which he blamed *her*.

She had tried to save money, hoping that soon she would be able to afford to leave and explore new possibilities. But it had been a hopeless task. Following George's death had come the discovery of more debts that he hadn't managed to pay, even with the money he'd made from selling the shop. Her savings had soon been swallowed up by them. And she had no hope of saving much more, given the meanly low pay Rik allowed her.

'I give you a fair wage,' he would say. 'You live here for nothing. If you worked somewhere else you'd have to pay for accommodation.'

It was true. Frantically she had hunted for another job, but hadn't been able to find one that paid enough to solve the problem. Now she felt trapped, and with no obvious way out she just had to hope for a miracle!

She showered and dressed carefully. She presented a picture of efficiency—ideal for the work that consumed her life—but her looks didn't please her. She considered herself far too plain.

She opened her laptop and logged on to her bank to check the state of her account. The result made her groan with despair. She had very little money, despite her attempts to live frugally.

Dispirited, she opened an astrology website, and read her prediction.

The fates are planning a startling new beginning for you. The sun in Jupiter will bring things you never anticipated, and decisions that will change your life.

In her dreams, she thought wryly. Last week it had said she was going to be a millionaire. And look how *that* had turned out.

She read the prediction again, trying to see it as the approach of the miracle she longed for, and then hurried downstairs and opened up the shop. She served a couple of customers, then spent some time looking around.

The shop had a variety of stock, including home wares and groceries. She often wished she could persuade Rik to show a little more imagination about the stock. But he had no sympathy for her ideas.

'This is a practical place, full of practical items,' he'd once told her sternly. 'You're too fanciful, Jackie. That's your trouble. You want life to be fun, and it isn't designed that way.'

'Not always fun,' she'd protested. 'Just a little bit of excitement now and then. I remember Daddy felt the same.'

'You father spent too much time looking for fun. It was his ruin.'

'*Something* ruined him…' She'd sighed. 'But I don't think it was that.'

'Get on with your work and stop wasting time.'

* * *

On the flight from Rome to London, Vittorio sat sunk in thought, wondering where the search for George Benton would finally lead him. Common sense told him he need not search at all. If he simply refused, who would ever know?

But his conscience would know. His promise had brought his father peace in his final moments. If he broke his word the knowledge would be with him for ever. And somewhere in his heart he sensed that his father's reproaches would always haunt him.

Everything had changed with Franco's death. He'd spoken of the pleasures of being Count Martelli, and Vittorio had soon discovered that it was true. The first time someone addressed him as 'Signor Conte' he had hardly been able to believe he'd heard correctly. His employees now treated him with deference, almost awe.

But his father had also spoken of other things— of the hidden problems behind the glamour, that the rest of the world knew nothing about. And here, too, he had been right.

Vittorio had gone through Franco's things, seeking clues about his father's past life and George Benton. He'd found a photograph of the two men together, which must have been taken during their meeting in England many years before.

How old would Benton be now? Middle-aged? At the height of his powers? Ready to take revenge on the family that had cheated him out of a fortune? He wasn't looking forward to their meeting, but there was no choice.

Franco's papers had also included a newspaper cutting, mentioning a shop called Benton's Market. There was a picture of a small, shabby-looking shop, and one of George Benton, looking older than in the other picture.

That was Vittorio's clue. He had a lead.

At the airport he hired a taxi and spent the journey studying a map of London. The area he sought was just north of the River Thames in the east of the city. As they approached the area Vittorio asked the driver, 'Is there a hotel near here?'

'There's one just around the corner. Mind you, it costs a lot.'

'Fine. Take me there.'

The hotel was pleasantly luxurious. He booked a room for the night, then went out to explore.

Almost at once he saw a corner shop with its sign proclaiming 'Benton's Market'. He took a deep breath, clenching his fists, vowing not to lose his nerve now.

Nearby was a small café, with tables outside. He found a seat, ordered some coffee and took out the photograph of Benton. From this angle he could see through the shop windows clearly enough to know if the man was there.

But time passed and there was no sign of him— only a young woman arranging stock in the main window. Much of it was already in place, but she was intent on reorganising it, giving it all her concentration.

He admired the woman's dedication and artistic flair. He would value such an employee himself, to work in the department store he owned and managed in Rome.

Suddenly he tensed as a man appeared from the rear of the shop. Could this be Benton? But he looked nothing like the picture. His face was thin and severe. His manner to the woman suggested ill temper. When he spoke Vittorio could just make out the words through the open door.

'*Must* you waste time faffing about over this? There's a pile of stuff at the back needs unpacking.'

'But I thought we agreed—' she began to say.

'Don't argue. Just do as I tell you. Get going.'

Looking exasperated, she retreated to the back of the shop.

Vittorio approached the shop, entering with the air of an eager customer.

'I'd like to buy some apples,' he said.

'We've got some here,' the man said. 'No— wait. They *were* over there. What has that stupid woman done with them?'

'I'd also like to talk to Mr Benton, please.'

The man glanced up, scowling. 'What do you want with him?' His tone became suspicious. 'You're not another debt collector, are you?'

'No, it's a personal matter.'

'Well, you can't see him. He's dead.'

'Dead?' Vittorio froze, feeling as though he'd heard a thunderclap. 'When?'

'A year ago. But his daughter still works here.'

'Was that her I saw? Can I talk to her?'

'You can, but not just yet. She's got work to do. You'll have to wait until she's finished for the day.'

Feeling depressed, Vittorio departed. Returning to the café he settled again to watch the shop, trying to get his thoughts in order. Everything he'd planned was in a shambles. He must talk to

Benton's daughter and just hope that she was a sensible woman who would accept financial compensation and let the matter end.

Throughout the afternoon he saw many customers go into the shop. The young woman dealt with them efficiently, always smiling and friendly. Every one of them bought something from her.

Benton's daughter was a natural saleswoman, it seemed.

He stayed there for four hours. He read the paper and then busied himself sending and receiving emails from his smartphone. The frustration of waiting was hard to endure but he forced himself. So much depended on this.

Inside the shop Jackie was working hard. Often she glanced out of the window, puzzled to see that the strange man was still there, sitting outside the café. She concluded that he must be a tourist, albeit a very well dressed one!

At last it was closing time. As she was preparing to leave, Rik arrived.

'Don't go yet,' he said, scowling. 'We need to have a talk about making new orders.'

'But I can't stay,' she protested. She gave him

a wry smile, saying, 'And, let's face it, you don't pay me enough to make me want to do overtime.'

'Don't be impertinent. I pay you a fair wage. If you did better I might pay you more.'

'It's not *my* fault profits are low,' she said indignantly. 'I don't think you're buying enough of the right stock.'

'And *I* don't think you're making a big enough effort,' he said coldly.

In his anger he spoke with a raised voice.

Vittorio, a few feet away, heard him through the open door. He rose and headed for the shop, from where Rik's grouchy voice could still be heard.

'I'm not asking. I'm telling you to stay where you are so we can discuss these orders.'

'*No!*' Jackie said furiously.

Once before she'd agreed to this demand and it had stretched to two hours, without so much as a penny being added to her wages.

'Now, look, Jackie—'

'We can talk tomorrow,' she said desperately.

Unable to bear any more, she fled blindly— and collided with a man entering through the front door. She began to fall, nearly taking him down with her.

'I'm sorry—' she gasped.

'No, *I'm* sorry,' Vittorio said, holding her firmly.

'Come back here,' Rik snapped, reaching out to take her arm in a fierce grip.

'Let me go!' she cried.

'I'll let you go when you do what you're paid to do.'

The last word ended on a yelp that burst from him at the feel of Vittorio's hand gripping his wrist.

'Let her go,' ordered Vittorio.

'Who the hell do you think you are?' Rik wailed.

'I said let her go, and you'd better do so if you know what's good for you.' Vittorio's voice was harsh and unrelenting.

Jackie felt Rik's painful grip on her arm loosen, until she was able to free herself.

A glance back at Rik showed he was scowling. She hurried away, following Vittorio, who put his arm protectively around her.

'Sorry about that,' he said. 'I didn't mean to get you in trouble with your boss.'

'Don't blame yourself.' She sighed. 'He's always like that.'

'I'm afraid I tripped you.'

'No, I tripped *you*. I wasn't looking where I was going.'

'But you stumbled. Are you sure you aren't hurt? I thought you might have twisted your ankle.'

'Just a little.'

'You should sit down. Let's go into the café.'

Once inside, he took her to a table in the corner, summoned the waiter and ordered coffee. When it was served he took a deep breath.

'Signorina—'

'My name's Jacqueline Benton. People call me Jackie.'

'Thank you—Jackie.'

'You called me *signorina*. Are you Italian?' She sounded hopeful.

'Yes, my name is Vittorio.'

She seemed pleased at the discovery. Smiling, she offered her hand. *'Buon giorno*, Vittorio.'

'Buon giorno, Jackie.'

'I really thank you for what you did—rescuing me from Rik.'

'He must be a nightmare to work for. But I guess you're out of a job now.'

'Probably not. You're right—he *is* a nightmare.

But things like that have happened before. He always apologises afterwards.'

'He *what*? I find that hard to believe.'

'So do I, in a way. But if I left it would be hard for him to find someone who'd put up with his horrible behaviour while knowing the place as well as I do.'

'So he knows how to act for his own benefit?' Vittorio said wryly.

'Oh, yes. Mind you, I suppose you could say that of everyone. We all do what suits us, and we don't really think about anyone else's feelings.'

He knew an uneasy moment. Was it possible that she suspected the truth about his arrival?

But she was smiling pleasantly, and he told himself not to panic.

'I find it hard to believe that of you,' he said gently.

'Oh, I can be selfish when it suits me.' She gave him a cheeky smile. 'You wouldn't *believe* the lengths I go to just to get my own way.'

He smiled back, charmed by her impish humour.

'I'll believe whatever you care to tell me,' he said. 'But you don't need to go to any great lengths. Just say what you want and I'll take care of it.'

That could be quite a temptation, she thought, remembering what she had read on the astrology site.

The fates are planning a startling new beginning for you. The sun in Jupiter will bring things you never anticipated...

Certainly she hadn't anticipated a charming, handsome man declaring himself at her service.

Watching her face, Vittorio managed to read her expression fairly well. He guessed she was trying decide how much fun they might have teasing each other.

And it might be *really* good fun, he thought. As well as humour there was a warmth in her eyes that tempted him to move closer.

'Rik said a man was asking after my father,' she said. 'Was that you?'

'Yes. I was sorry to hear that he was dead.'

'Why are you looking for him?'

Vittorio hesitated, sensing the approach of danger. Suddenly he was reluctant to disturb the delightful atmosphere between them.

'My own father knew him several years ago,' he said carefully.

'How did they meet? Did your father try to sell him some Italian goods for the shop?'

'No, he wasn't a salesman. He was Count Martelli.'

He waited for her to react with delight to hearing his status, as he was used to, but she only said ironically, 'A count? You're the son of a *count*? Are you kidding?'

'No, I'm not. And, since my father has died, I *am* the Count.'

She burst into a delicious chuckle. 'You must think I'm so gullible.'

'Why don't you believe me?'

'Because my father never once mentioned knowing a *count*—or even admitted meeting one. I just can't imagine that my father was ever friends with an aristocrat, not when we were so poor.'

'Was he really poor? He managed to start his own business.'

'He borrowed a lot of money to buy the shop. And it was a big mistake. He never really made the profit he needed, and we always lived on the edge of poverty.'

'That must have been a very sad life for you,' Vittorio said uneasily.

'Not for me as much as for him. It destroyed his marriage to my mother. She left him for another man. For years Daddy and I had only each other. I adored him. He was a lovely man…sweet-natured, generous. I went to work in the shop, to help him. It wasn't the life I'd planned—I'd dreamed of going to university. But I couldn't abandon him. And in the end he was forced to sell. Rik beat him down on the price, but he offered me a job and let us go on living there. I did all I could for Daddy, but it wasn't enough. A couple of years ago he had a heart attack.'

Vittorio dropped his head, staring at the floor. In his worst nightmares he'd never imagined anything as bad as this. If George Benton had received the money that should have been his everything would have been different for him. He might even be alive now.

What would she say when he told her?

He clenched his fists, trying to find the courage to do the right thing.

But his courage failed him, and to his relief the waiter appeared.

'We're about to close, sir.'

'Then I guess we have to go,' he said hurriedly, trying not to sound too relieved.

It was dark outside. He walked Jackie to the shop door and waited, wondering if she would invite him in. But she only said, 'I'm glad we met. It was nice to have coffee.'

'Yes, it was. Jackie…' He hesitated, uncertain how to go on.

'Yes?'

'Nothing. Perhaps we can—see each other again. I'd like to talk.'

'So would I. Tomorrow?'

'I'll look in.'

She went inside, locking the door behind her. For some moments Vittorio stood in silence, trying to come to a troubling decision.

He should have told her everything, but he knew the truth would hurt her greatly. He felt that in his heart, and flinched from striking that blow.

He'd planned every step of the way how he would confront George Benton, explain, apologise, and draw a line under it. Instead he found

himself confronted with a woman whose sweetness and vulnerability touched his heart. And the
truth was he didn't know how to respond.

After standing there hopelessly for several
minutes he turned and hurried away into the
darkness.

CHAPTER TWO

NEXT MORNING VITTORIO awoke early. The clock said half past five and suddenly there seemed no point in staying in bed. Showering and dressing quickly, he headed straight out.

It felt good to enjoy the fresh air and the fast-growing light. But then he saw something that alarmed him. A young woman walking away in the distance. It was hard to be certain of details, but she looked strangely like…

Jackie.

Wanting to be sure, he hurried after her, but she turned a corner out of sight.

Cursing, he ran desperately through the streets. He didn't know London at all. It was hopeless, he thought frantically when he found himself by the River Thames. She must be walking along the embankment—but in which direction?

Then luck was with him. After a hundred yards he could see her, sitting on a bench, staring out over the water. He moved closer, struck by the way she seemed sunk in another world. It reminded him of himself the night before.

He stayed silent, unsure whether it was right for him to disturb her, but after a moment she glanced up.

'Vittorio? What are you doing up this early?' she asked.

'I couldn't sleep so I thought I'd stretch my legs. How are you this morning, Jackie? Are you worried about facing Rik today?'

'I'm fine—honestly.'

'Forgive me, but I don't think you are.' He lifted her chin with his fingers, looking at her face. 'You've been crying.'

'Just a little.'

He put his arms round her, overtaken by a desire to care for her. Protectiveness was a feeling he'd seldom, if ever, known before, and now it was almost alarming. He had to tell her something that would break her heart, and suddenly he wasn't sure that he could do it.

'Hold on to me,' he whispered. 'It'll be all right.'

'Sometimes I think things will *never* be all

right,' she said. 'I'm sorry to dump all this on you, but I can't talk about Daddy without—'

'Without remembering all the bad things that happened to him?'

'I don't know why, Vittorio, but I feel I could tell you anything.'

She looked up again and the sight of her vulnerable face swept him with a desire to kiss her. He yielded—but only to lay his lips on her forehead.

'Do you want to tell me any more?' he murmured.

'You can't want to hear such a terrible story,' she said.

She was more right than she could imagine, he thought wretchedly. But he owed it to her to listen.

'You can tell me *anything*, Jackie.'

She brushed the tears aside from her face. 'I don't really know what to say… It isn't my tragedy.'

'In a way it is. You lost too. You wanted to go to university. What did you want to study?'

'I wanted to study languages. They just seem to come easily to me.'

He regarded her wryly.

'Buon per te, signorina. La maggior parte delle persone non possono far fronte con le lingue.'

He spoke in Italian. His words meant, 'Good for you *signorina*. Most people can't cope with languages.'

'Italian is the language I manage best,' she said. 'I took a few classes at night school, because we were planning to take a holiday there together. My father longed to travel to Italy. He'd been there once as a young man.'

'Did he tell you a lot about his visit?'

'Yes, he said it was such fun.'

'Did he never mention meeting my father?' he asked.

'He mentioned an Italian friend, but said nothing at all about him being a *count*! They met in Italy and then again in England a few weeks later. From what Daddy said I gather they got on really well and enjoyed each other's company.'

Vittorio nodded. 'Yes I remember Papà saying something like that—I gather they had quite a few adventures together whilst he was there.'

'Daddy said things like that too. He had such a lovely time with his Italian friend. Only then—' She checked herself.

'Then?' Vittorio said tensely. He had an uneasy feeling that he knew what was coming.

'Then suddenly it was all over. One day they were close buddies—the next day his friend disappeared. He left a note but it didn't say much. Just *Goodbye my friend. Franco*'. No address, nothing. Daddy couldn't contact him and he never heard from him again. It left him very unhappy after what they'd been to each other.'

'He told you that? Didn't he tell you any more about who the man was?'

'No, just that his name was Franco. If he'd known more he'd have told me, I'm sure. Maybe your father never let him know that he was a count?'

'Maybe…' he murmured.

Their eyes met, and what Jackie saw took her breath away. There was an intensity in his gaze as though nothing but herself existed in the world. It was something she'd never seen in any man's eyes before, and she became suddenly conscious of the soft thump of her own heartbeat.

'Jackie—' Vittorio checked himself, unsure how to continue. This was taking more courage than he had anticipated.

'What's the matter?' she asked. 'Are you all right?'

'I'm fine—but there's something I must—'

She felt a sudden sense of brilliant illumination—as though the clouds had parted on a rainy day. She'd hardly dared to hope that the vibrant attraction that possessed her possessed him too, but now she let herself wonder if perhaps it did.

A memory returned to her. That astrology prediction had said, *The fates are planning a startling new beginning for you. The sun in Jupiter will bring things you never anticipated, and decisions that will change your life.*

It was happening. This was the great moment that fate had planned for her. Now surely he would tell her how their meeting had affected his heart, and that was something her own heart longed to know.

She clasped his hand between hers.

'Whatever you have to say, I know I'll like it,' she breathed. 'We've understood each other from the first moment, and—'

'Yes…' he murmured. 'Yes—*yes*—'

He knew the next few minutes would be tense, but something in her seemed to reach out to him, drawing him into a circle of warmth such as he'd never known before. It was what he needed most in all the world, and he knew a moment of fear lest his revelation ruin things between them.

He raised her hands and brushed his lips against them. 'I hope so much that you're right,' he said. 'But you can't imagine—'

'I think I can. Daddy always said you had to be ready for the unexpected.' She met his eyes, her own full of happiness and hope. 'And I'm ready for anything. Say it, Vittorio, and you might like my answer.'

He drew a sharp breath. Now the moment had come when he must find the courage to tell her everything.

But the sight of her eyes shining up at him caused his courage to fail. Suddenly he could see how that light would fade when she knew the terrible truth behind her father's suffering. The thought of her pain made him shudder, and he knew he could not force himself to speak.

'I have to go,' he said uneasily.

'What? But—'

'I'm expecting an important phone call. I have to get back to the hotel.'

He rose to his feet and she followed him reluctantly. Suddenly a moment filled with magic had dissolved into nothing, leaving her desolate.

As they walked back beside the river it began to drizzle.

'Better get back quickly, before it really starts to rain,' he said.

They hurried the rest of the way, until they reached the shop.

'I'll see you again soon,' he said. 'We'll talk then. Take care of yourself.'

Then he fled, devoured by thoughts whose bitterness was aimed accusingly at himself. He was no better than a coward!

His own words came back to him.

You can never tell what fate has in store for you.

It was more true than he could have dreamed. His plan for this meeting had never included the desire to hold her, comfort her, protect her—do anything rather than hurt her. It had overtaken him without warning, reducing him to helplessness. And there was no turning back.

Inside the shop, Jackie hurried up the stairs and looked out of the window in time to see Vittorio vanish around the corner.

She sighed sadly. It was obvious what had

happened. He'd been about to kiss her but had changed his mind at the last moment.

Did he want her or not? He had seemed to be trying to tell her something without words. Had she misunderstood him? But he *had* seemed on the verge of telling her something.

What could it possibly be?

She busied herself opening up the shop. Saturdays were always busy. But somehow she couldn't get stop thinking about him. He was there in her mind, his eyes glowing with a look that made her heart beat faster.

Next day was Sunday, which meant the shop was closed. Fearful of missing her, Vittorio hurried there early. He'd lost his nerve the day before, but he couldn't risk losing it again.

A window opened above him and a voice said coolly, 'Good morning, Vittorio.'

Jackie was looking down at him.

'Morning!' he cried, smiling brightly. 'Can you come down?'

'I'm not sure—'

'Please, Jackie, it's important. We really have to talk.'

'We could have talked yesterday.'

'Please.'

'All right. I'll just be a moment.'

She hurried down, full of hope that her tense wait would be over. He seemed to have come close and then retreated, and now she couldn't bear any more. It *must* be the dream she'd longed for. They had known each other such a little time, but what did time matter when their hearts reached out to each other?

Perhaps his feelings were stronger than he'd known before, which was why he feared expressing them. But she would open her arms and her heart to him and they would both know happiness.

As soon as she appeared downstairs he put his arm about her shoulders.

'Let's have some breakfast in the café. It's nice and comfortable in there.'

'And we can talk,' she said eagerly.

When they were settled she waited for him to speak, but again he felt silent, as though attacked by doubt at the last moment. Her heart sank. Her hopes had risen so high. She couldn't bear to lose them again.

'Vittorio, please tell me,' she said. 'Whatever is on your mind I can tell it's important.'

'Yes, it is…' he said hesitantly.

'Then please be brave and say it. Are you afraid of what I'll say?'

'I might be,' he said. 'I don't think you can imagine—'

She touched his face. 'Tell me, Vittorio. Let's get it out between us and then tell each other how we feel.'

'Yes,' he murmured. 'You're right. Do you re-member—?'

'Remember?'

'How we talked about our fathers yesterday.'

'Yes, I remember, but—'

'I should have told you then. It's a terrible story, Jackie, but I have to tell you. Your father once placed a bet that won a million pounds.'

'But that can't be true! He'd have told me—we'd never have been in the situation we found ourselves in if that had been the case.'

'He didn't know. My father and yours were out together one night. Your father got tipsy, and he was dozing when the results were announced. When he awoke my *papà* had taken the winnings and kept them.'

Jackie had a terrible feeling of having crash-landed. The words reeled in her head. Only one thing was clear.

This wasn't what she'd expected to hear.

'What on earth are you saying?' she demanded. 'You *can't* mean that he didn't tell Daddy he'd won? That would be dishonest, and surely—'

'It was the only dishonest thing he ever did, and it tormented him. He told me about it just before he died.'

'Is this—this what you've been trying to say?' she stammered.

'Yes, it took me this long to pluck up the courage to tell you that my family has damaged yours. I'm sure you'll find it hard to forgive. Right at this minute you probably hate me.'

That was closer to the truth than he could possibly know. As her dreams collapsed, leaving her in the middle of a desert, she felt a terrifying rage begin to take her over.

'There's something else I have to tell you,' Vittorio said. 'I'm not sure how it will make you feel.'

'Try me,' she whispered, with a faint flicker of renewed hope.

'Papà made me promise to find your father and sort things out.'

'Sort things out? What do you mean by that?'

'I planned to give him the money Papà took from him. A million pounds. I hoped it would make everything all right.'

She stared at him, barely able to believe what she was hearing.

'You hoped *what*?' she said furiously. 'You really hoped things could be made *"all right"* after so many years? After Daddy suffered so much from poverty and it made his wife abandon him? After the way he died in despair? You can't give him your money *now*.'

'But I can give it to you.'

'You think that will make his suffering *all right*?'

'I didn't mean it that way,' Vittorio said tensely.

'Oh, yes, you did. You think money can solve everything—but when a man's dead it can't solve anything at all. You don't understand that, do you? Hand over a cheque and everything's settled! Maybe that's true in business, but not in real life. But you don't know anything about real life.'

'Jackie, please—let me explain. I only want to—'

'You only want to make yourself feel good.'

'I don't think money solves everything, but I'd like to pay the debt my family owes.

'This is a con. Do you *really* expect me to believe that you can hand over a million pounds, just like that?'

'You think I don't have that much? You're wrong. My father didn't waste the million he gained.'

'You mean the million he *stole*,' she raged.

'Very well—he stole it. But he wanted to pay it back. He invested it successfully, so that it made several more millions. I can give you back every penny—plus a few thousand for interest.'

'Oh, you think it's so easy, don't you? I wouldn't take money from you if I was starving. This conversation is at an end.' She stood up. 'And don't you dare follow me.'

He'd reached out a hand to stop her, but something fierce in her manner made him draw back.

'Please—' he began.

'No. Don't you understand? *No!*'

She fled, fearful lest her true feelings become too plain. Instead of the loving emotion she'd hoped for he'd offered her *money*. If she'd stayed a moment longer she was afraid she might have done something violent.

Her departure left Vittorio in a state of total confusion and misery. Nothing had worked out as he'd intended. He'd failed to fulfil his father's dying wish. Guilt tore at him.

He paid his bill and went out into the street, walking back in the direction of the shop. There was no sign of her.

There was nothing to do but return to the hotel and do some serious thinking about what he was going to do next.

But he found that serious thinking was very little help in a situation he didn't understand.

The rest of Jackie's day and night was tormented. The incredible events of the morning whirled through her brain, and at the end of the day— even though she was exhausted and wrung out when she finally got to bed—she couldn't sleep. Instead she sat up in bed and opened the laptop she always kept with her.

She did a search on 'Count Martelli'. She was half ready to learn that he didn't exist, that the whole thing had been a con, and for a moment it seemed that her suspicions were correct. The picture that appeared on the screen was of a man in his sixties.

He's lying, she thought furiously. *That's the real Count.*

But then she saw the text.

Count Franco Martelli, taken just before his death four weeks ago. His heir is his son, Vittorio Martelli, latest in a line stretching back five hundred years.

She clicked the link marked 'Count Vittorio Martelli' and and at once saw a photograph of the man she recognised. There was no doubt.

Her temper surged once more at the memory of Vittorio trying to pay her off to assuage his family's guilt. But had she been too hasty? Had she let her temper get the better of her once again?

Vivid in her mind was the memory of her father's suffering. He'd tried to put on a brave face for her sake, but he hadn't always been able to manage it. Often she had found him in tears. He'd smiled and reassured her, but over time she had come to understand the problems. Her heart had broken for him. She had become his comforter, intent on giving him some kind of happiness.

But the last year of her father's life had been the saddest she had ever known. She still wept when she remembered his suffering.

Vittorio thought money was the answer to everything!

And yet she knew there was another reason for her rage. When she remembered how her hopes of winning Vittorio's feelings had risen, and then been smashed to the ground, she felt capable of murder.

He had just been playing a game until he had what suited him. He hadn't spared a thought as to what it was doing to *her.*

So accept the money, said a voice in her head. *He offered you a million—more than a million with interest.*

Because he thought it would put right what his father had done. If he wasn't such a heartless monster he'd know that nothing could *ever* make it right.

What would her father have done? If he were still alive it would be so different. Then of course they would have accepted the money. It would have been his due. But now he was gone would it be right for her to accept it on his behalf?

She closed the laptop and went back to bed. At last she managed to nod off, sinking into a deep and dreamless sleep.

* * *

Vittorio's night had also been troubled. He'd fallen asleep easily, but found his dreams haunted by Jackie's contempt until they were practically nightmares that woke him in a cold sweat.

He rose out of bed. He had no desire to go back to sleep lest the alarming female return to torment him. Day was breaking and he felt the need of a fresh air. Dressing hastily, he went downstairs and out into the street.

His thoughts were full of the promise he'd made to his beloved father. Come what might he *had* to make this right—for everyone's sake.

Almost at once the shop came in sight. It was time for it to be open, so he went closer and looked through the glass door, but he could see no sign of anyone. Moving quietly, he opened the door and slipped inside. At once he heard the sound of voices coming from deep within. One was Jackie's, and the other he recognised as the weasely boss who had appeared during his first visit. His voice was raised in annoyance.

'Jackie, you're *mad*. You should have got all you could out of the Count and then invested in this place. I could do with some money to cover the debts. You could have helped me out and you just turned it down? How could you be so *stupid*?'

She replied in a voice filled with rage that reminded Vittorio of the way she'd spoken to him with equal fury during last night.

'You think I should have taken his money and used it for *your* convenience?' she raged at Rik. 'I'm not *that* stupid.'

Vittorio stepped a little closer, careful to keep out of sight but wanting to hear everything.

'You just can't recognise reality when it's under your nose,' came Rik's reply. 'You had the chance of a fortune. You could have taken it. But perhaps your fantasies are fixed on something else.'

'What does that mean?'

'It's *him*, isn't it? You refused his money because you're hoping for a better offer! You think you can lure him into marriage, but you're wasting your time. A man like that wouldn't marry *you* in a million years.'

'And I wouldn't marry *him* in a million years. He's cold—and arrogant enough to think that money can solve anything.'

Vittorio made a wry face. A wise man would have slipped away at this moment, but he didn't feel wise. He felt as though Jackie had seized him and was holding him at her mercy in whirls of confusion.

'It can solve a great deal,' he heard Rik say. 'It could pay a lot of my debts—many of which are *your* fault.'

'How can you say that?'

'If you did a better job this shop would be doing well, instead of sinking into debt.'

'The shop was in a bad way when my father sold it to you. That's how you got it so cheap. I heard you—beating him down on the price when he was too weak to fight you.'

'Don't try to blame me for your father's failings. Luckily it's not too late. You've still got time to find this Italian Count and tell him you'll take the money.'

'You think I'd—? You're mad.'

'I'm *telling* you to do it.'

'And I'm telling *you* to go to hell.'

'I warn you, Jackie, you're walking a very fine line. Perhaps I'd better see him myself—'

'Perhaps you should,' Vittorio said, stepping out so that they could see him.

Rik noticed him first, and the shock on his face alerted Jackie, so that she looked behind her, also appalled at the discovery.

Rik assumed a severe manner. 'We have business to discuss,' he said.

'The only business we have is for you to listen to what I have to say,' Vittorio said bluntly. 'For you—not a penny.'

'But you have a debt to pay,' Rik squealed.

'Not to *you*.'

'Jackie, tell him,' Rik whined. 'Tell him he's got to pay you what he owes you.'

Jackie looked intently at Vittorio, but did not speak.

'Do it now,' Rik snapped. 'Let me hear you say it.'

'I have nothing to say,' she replied coldly. 'The Count's debt is impossible to repay.' She met Vittorio's gaze and said emphatically, *'Ever!'*

Rik looked from one to the other, scowling.

'So *that's* it,' he raged. 'You two are in this together. As soon as I'm out of earshot you'll take the money and cut me out.'

'You can't be cut out because you were never *in*,' Jackie said fiercely. 'You bought this business fair and square, and any debts are now your responsibility. Besides, I will never take a penny of his money.'

'You're insane!' Rik seethed. 'What kind of

fool turns down that sort of money? Well, if money's of no importance to you then you won't be needing this job. *Or* the accommodation I've provided for you. You're fired. I'll give you one hour to clear out your stuff from upstairs.'

Rik stormed out, pausing at the front door.

'One hour!' he yelled. 'I mean it.'

Then he was gone, slamming the door behind him.

Vittorio turned swiftly to Jackie. 'Good riddance.' he said. 'Forget him. He isn't worth bothering with.'

Jackie was shaken, but determined to maintain her dignity. 'How long were you there, listening?'

'I came to see you and arrived just as you were telling him what had happened.'

'I never meant to tell him, but he made me so angry that I said it to knock the smile off his face. I could have strangled him.' She gave a bitter laugh. 'I'd have enjoyed that.'

'Don't worry. He's bound to give you another excuse. He's a pig, Jackie, and you're better off without him.'

'But this isn't just my *job*. I've lived here all my life and now I've lost my home, too.'

'Then we must find you another one. Get packing and we'll be out of here—fast.'

'I've nowhere to go.'

'Trust me to arrange that.'

She knew an instinct to rebel against him. This catastrophe had happened only because he'd come to England and caused trouble. Now she'd lost her job and her home, and he was to blame.

But was he really? If she hadn't been silly enough to tell Rik about the money this wouldn't have happened. When was she going to learn to control her temper?

Never, she thought fiercely.

'Let's get you out of here,' Vittorio said. He took her arm and ran up the stairs with her and began opening drawers and cupboards, working hard to help her.

'Is that your only suitcase?' he asked, regarding the one she had produced.

'Yes, but I've got some plastic bags.'

Luckily the bags proved enough to take her few possessions.

'Anything else?' he asked at last.

'No, that's all.'

'You have nothing else?' he asked, looking astonished.

'This is all I need,' she said defiantly.

He gave her an odd look, as though wondering what madness had made her refuse his money when she seemed to own so little, but all he said was, 'Then let's go.'

She looked around nervously as they went downstairs, but there was no sign of Rik.

'Where are we going?' she asked as they went out into the street.

'I'm staying in the Davien Hotel, a couple of streets away. We'll get you a room there for to-night, then make our plans.'

She knew the hotel. It had a reputation as being costly.

'I don't think it's quite the right place for me,' she said uneasily.

'If you're worried about the money, don't be. I'm paying. I landed you in this mess and it's my responsibility to get you out.'

Suddenly she recalled Rik's warning to her. He'd suggested that Vittorio was hoping to lure Jackie into bed with the empty promise of a great fortune.

Suddenly she was uneasy. Was that why Vittorio was taking her to his hotel at his own expense? Did he mean her to share his bed?

Only recently that thought would have excited her. Vittorio attracted her powerfully. The thought of lying with him in bed would have been a pleasure. But now everything was different. Was he trustworthy? Could she be sure?

A short walk brought them to the hotel. Vittorio went to Reception and chatted with the woman there as she typed something onto the keyboard. Nodding to her, he headed back to Jackie.

'I've managed to secure you a room on the second floor.'

He escorted her upstairs, leading her to a door for which he had the key. She held her breath.

But when the door opened she knew she'd done him an injustice. There was only one single bed.

'Th-thank you,' she stammered.

'If you need me I'm three doors along the corridor.'

He departed at once, leaving her standing alone, trying to take in everything that had happened. Only yesterday she had quarrelled with this man, and today he had come to her rescue and she had accepted his help gladly.

It doesn't make any sense, she mused.

But nothing had made sense since she'd met him. Perhaps nothing ever would again.

He returned just as she finished putting her things away.

'They do a good lunch here,' he said. 'I'll have some sent up.'

'Couldn't we eat downstairs in the restaurant?'

'Do I make you feel nervous, Jackie? Are you afraid to be alone with me?'

'Of course not,' she said uneasily. 'I have no feelings about you one way or the other, actually,' she lied bravely.

'So you didn't mean it when you said you wouldn't marry me in a million years? Or the bit about me being cold and arrogant and a person who thinks money can solve anything?'

For a moment it was as though her worst nightmares were coming true. But then she saw he was grinning, and that his eyes were full of friendly humour.

'Forget it,' he said. 'People say things in the heat of the moment. And it's not far different from what you said to me yesterday. But it's time we drew a line under that. We have to work matters out between us and be friends—if that's possible.'

It was still embarrassing to know that he'd

heard her, but his unexpected humour made it bearable.

'So—can I have some food sent up?' he asked.

'Are you asking my permission?'

Again he gave her a cheeky grin. 'Isn't that what you prefer a man to do?'

'Stop trying to make me sound like a bully.'

'Not a bully. Just a woman who knows her own mind—as Rik would tell us after the way you stood up to him. He's a nasty bully, but you really dealt with him.'

'Yes—and that was so successful that now I've got to start looking for another job and a home.'

'But where? You'll never get another job around here. He'll make sure of that.'

She groaned, recognising that Vittorio was right. Rik would spread the word that she was unreliable, destroying her prospects.

'I still feel that I owe you any help I can persuade you to accept,' Vittorio said.

'You have a job to offer me?'

'Not here, but in Italy. I could find many opportunities for you there. Why not come back with me?'

CHAPTER THREE

JACKIE STARED AT him in disbelief. 'Italy? Did I hear right?'

'Dead right. I want you to work for me in my family's department store in Rome. Your talents will be valuable.'

'But I've only ever worked in a little shop. I'd be useless in a department store.'

'Not in our glass and china section. It's a new department, and it isn't doing brilliantly because nobody really understands it. But you could bring it to life and make it profitable.'

'According to Rik, I was lousy at making profits.'

'Were you? Or did *he* make a lot of stupid decisions?'

'Yes, he buys all the wrong stuff.'

'So I can rely on you to buy all the *right* stuff?'

'Mightn't the language be a problem? I never got to finish my Italian course at night school. I had to stop when Daddy became ill.'

'A lot of people there speak English. Some of our customers are tourists, and your English would be a blessing to them. Your Italian seems already pretty good, and you can work to improve it.'

'It's very kind of you—' she began uneasily.

'No, it isn't. I'm not being kind. I'm a businessman and I'm doing what any sensible businessman does—turning the situation to my own advantage. I could make a lot of money out of you, and I'm not passing up the chance to do that.'

'But how—?'

'You won't just have that one department. I want you to cast your expert eye over the whole store and tell me how it looks to you—because that will tell me how it looks to our customers. Tourists are profitable, and you can help me attract plenty of them. And it could open some new doors for you, Jackie. I'll pay you a decent wage—far more than Rik paid you—and you'll have a position of authority.'

Authority. The word seemed to sing in her ears. This would truly be a new, more satisfying life— exactly what she had longed for. Again she had the mysterious feeling that Vittorio could read her mind.

'Authority?' she echoed. 'Do you really mean that?'

'You'd be in charge of your department. You'd have a team that would take your orders. Or don't you feel up to giving orders?'

'Oh, yes, I do. That was always my problem with Rik. And with my father too sometimes. He complained that I argued with him too much.' She gave a brief laugh.

'Don't worry. When you're working for me you can give all the orders you want. I'll make it clear to the team that *you're* the boss. You need never fear another bully like Rik.'

It sounded too good to be true, she thought, trying to suppress a flicker of confusion. Knowing the terrible truth about how her father had been treated had made hostility flare between them, but there were other feelings too—some warmer, some interested, all confusing.

But what else could she do? Where else was there for her to go? What other life was possible for her? It was as if all other doors had slammed shut and fate was driving her irresistibly into this man's power.

Surely she could take advantage of the situation, just as *he* planned to do?

Here was a chance to learn new skills and gain new experiences that might open up a world of fresh opportunities for her.

'All right,' she said in a daze. 'I'll go to Italy with you.'

'Good thinking. I knew I could rely on you.'

She ventured to say, 'You mean because I've agreed with you?'

'What else? That's my definition of good thinking. So, now there's nothing to hold you back we can go tomorrow. I'll book two tickets.'

After booking the tickets Vittorio ordered a meal and a bottle of wine from room service.

'After this I must attend to some business matters. I suggest you relax for the rest of the afternoon, and then I think we should both get an early night,' he said, adding in a teasing voice, 'In our separate rooms, I promise.'

'Stop teasing,' she said cheerfully. 'I wasn't thinking that.'

'Good. Then we can both relax.'

'Of course. We agree to be friends. That's all.'

'Friends…' he mused. 'What kind of friends? Best friends?'

'We'll have to wait and see.'

She was right. Friendship was their only hope. Had she really feared lest he come to her door? After their argument the day before he could well believe that she didn't want him. His own feelings for her were less clear.

Officially they were enemies, and his instinct to protect her was troublesome.

She was becoming important to him in ways that confused him. Perhaps soon he would understand them. For the moment he preferred to wait and see what fate had in store.

He lifted his glass of wine in her direction.

'Here's to you,' he said. 'You don't know how much I'm going to rely on you.'

And it was true, he thought. She didn't.

It was a quiet meal, with very little talk. Instinctively they both knew that for the moment enough had been said. Perhaps too much.

At the earliest moment they finished eating.

'And now I really must get on with some work. I'll head back to my room, but if you think of anything else you need today please call through.'

He bade her a polite good day, and left.

Returning to his room, he recalled something

he'd meant to say to her, and hurried back to see her.

A surprise awaited him. He looked out into the corridor just in time to see her getting into the elevator and the doors closing.

Where on earth could she be going? he thought frantically. Surely not to talk to Rik?

There was no hope of catching up with the elevator. He went to his window and looked down. There she was, walking away along the road, and then turning through a large gate that he knew led to a church.

Every cautious instinct told him to stay where he was—not to follow her. But something about Jackie always overcame caution.

In a moment he was out of the door, hurrying until he reached the church gate.

Inside was a cemetery. As he watched she approached a tombstone and knelt before it. He was too far away to make out the name, but he could hear Jackie saying urgently, 'I'm sorry, Daddy. I really am.'

So this was Benton's grave, and she had come here to talk to him. Vittorio backed away, unwilling to invade her privacy, but he couldn't help hearing her next words.

'I don't really trust him. I'd like to, but he doesn't understand what a terrible thing was done to you, and that makes him almost as much of an enemy as his father. But I must go to Italy. I'll come back, I promise. Only forgive me. Please, *please* forgive me.'

As watched she pressed her lips to the stone, then leaned against it, sobbing.

Torn by the instinct to comfort her, he took a step closer—but stopped just in time. Whatever happened, she mustn't know he was there. He had an unnerving feeling…as though he'd been suddenly stranded on a desert island. He hadn't expected this, and the sensation of being caught unprepared was alarming.

He backed off and hurried away, haunted by her words—

I don't trust him... Almost as much of an enemy as his father...

If that was how she thought of him he supposed he couldn't blame her. But it hurt more than he would have expected.

Back at the hotel, he returned to his room and went to the window, hoping to see her return. But hours passed with no sign of her and his heart sank. Where had she vanished to *now*?

What trouble might she have fallen into? Had she changed her mind about accompanying him to Italy?

Then a noise from the corridor made him hurry outside. She was there, turning the key in her lock.

'There you are,' he said with relief.

'Were you looking for me? I'm sorry I vanished. I just had to— Well, never mind.'

He hesitated. All his cautious instincts warned him to keep the secret, but the need to be honest with her was greater.

At last he said, 'You just had to say goodbye to your father.'

She stared at him. 'How do you know?'

'I saw you.'

'But how?'

'I followed you to the cemetery.'

She gasped with outrage. 'You *followed* me? How *dare* you?'

She stormed into her room and tried to close the door, but he reached out to keep it open.

'Let me come in,' he said.

'I'd rather you didn't. In fact I'd rather you vanished off the face of the earth.'

'Well, I'm sure you'll eventually think of a way

of making that happen. But for the moment we need to talk. Let me in, Jackie. *Please.*'

Furiously, she turned away. He followed her in, closing the door behind him.

'Don't judge me, Jackie—please. I'm not stalking you. I followed you because I'm concerned about you. You seemed so lonely, walking, and when you reached the grave...' He paused, feeling desperate. 'You cried so terribly. I wanted to take you in my arms and comfort you. I didn't because I knew you'd be angry that I was there. I went away. I wasn't sure that was the right thing to do, but I don't seem to get anything right these days. The more I try, the more wrong I get it. But I'm glad I was with you for a few minutes. I think I understand you better now.'

He saw a strange, slightly puzzled look come into her face.

'Yes, that surprises you, doesn't it?' he said. 'I'm the last person you'd expect to understand you.'

'People don't easily understand other people,' she murmured.

'But I think we manage it. We must talk about that another time. For now, please just tell me that you believe I meant no harm and you forgive me.'

'All right,' she said reluctantly. 'I realise you didn't mean it badly.'

'And I'm forgiven? Please Jackie. Let me hear you say it. *Please.*'

She drew a sharp breath, stunned by the desperation in his voice and the intensity in his eyes. There was no way she could refuse this man anything he asked for.

'I forgive you,' she said.

'And you mean it?'

'Yes—*yes*—'

'As long as you *do* mean it. Things could so easily go wrong between us—but we won't let that happen. Best if you go to bed now and have a good night's sleep. Tomorrow will be a busy day. Goodnight.'

'Goodnight.'

Before leaving he turned to look back at her once more. Jackie tried to understand his expression, but there was something about it that confused her.

Nor was that the only thing about him so unexpected that she could hardly believe it. The way he'd almost begged her for forgiveness had startled her, revealing a side of him she'd never suspected.

She was glad to lie down. She needed sleep, but for some reason it didn't come. It was alarming that he'd been there while she spoke to her father. Had he heard her say that she didn't trust him?

She lay still, listening for the sound of his footsteps outside, wondering if they would return to her door. But nothing happened.

At last the silence seemed to overwhelm her and she fell asleep.

As Vittorio had said, they rose early next day and were soon ready to leave.

'You won't be insulted if I pay your bill, will you?' he asked as they went downstairs.

'Would it make any difference if I was?'

He grinned. 'Not the slightest.'

'Then I'd better give in—until I find a way to make you sorry.'

'I'll look forward to that,' he said ironically.

She watched as he went to the reception desk and paid. Then all was ready and they headed for the front door.

But as soon as it was open she saw something that made her stop, frozen with dismay.

'Oh, no!' she groaned.

'What is it?' Vittorio asked. 'Ah, I see. *Him!*'

Rik was standing there, barring their way, his face full of spiteful hilarity.

'So there you are!' he jeered. 'Just as I thought—you stupid woman!'

'You told me to leave so I went,' she said coldly.

'Yes, you went running to *him*. Think you're going to be a countess, do you? Don't kid yourself! He's playing a clever game to stop you suing him for the money his family stole. He'll use you, then throw you out.'

'The only one who's being thrown out is you,' Vittorio said coldly.

Rik gave contemptuous laugh. 'Don't tell me you're taken in by her—? *Argh!*'

The scream was dragged from him by the feel of Vittorio's hand about his neck.

'I know all I need to know about this lady,' Vittorio said harshly. 'But let me tell you something about myself. I'm a man who won't tolerate an insult to a friend, and who'll do anything necessary to make someone sorry they caused trouble. Do you understand me?'

'Yes…' Rik choked.

'Then get out of here while you still can. Otherwise I might do something we'd both regret.'

He released Rik, who staggered away, looking terrified. He gave one last appalled glance at Jackie. Then he fled.

'Are you all right?' Vittorio asked her.

'Yes—fine—thank you.'

In truth she was far from all right. She'd seen yet another side of Vittorio—one that shocked her. The look in his eyes had been that of a man who would go to any lengths to punish someone who had defied him. She knew it had been in her defence, but that couldn't ease her horror.

'Would you really have hurt him?' she whispered.

'No, of course not. But I had to make him believe that I would. Scare someone enough and you don't need to do anything else to them. Being frank. Isn't that something you've tried yourself.'

'Now and then,' she admitted. 'Not violently, but—'

'But making him believe you know something he doesn't want you to know? I'd give a lot to know how often you've used *that* one.'

'You'll just have to wonder,' she said lightly.

'Congratulations. You're as bad as I am. Shake.'

He held out his hand.

Laughing, she took it. 'I'll never be as bad as you are,' she said. 'But I'm working on it.'

'Perhaps he was right about one thing. *Should* I be afraid of you suing me?'

'Of course not. How can I?'

'I've admitted the theft.'

'It was your father's theft, not yours. And there were no witnesses when you told me. You could just deny it and there'd be nothing I could do.'

'Maybe Rik overheard me?'

'Don't believe anything Rik says—especially that nonsense about me wanting to be a countess.'

'Of course. I know you wouldn't marry me in a million years. I heard you say so yourself, remember?'

'Look, about that… I really am sorry—'

'Don't be sorry. You're not the first woman who's said that about me.' He grinned wryly. 'As you can probably imagine.'

'I'm not going to be tricked into answering that!'

'Very shrewd. I can see you're a real discovery.'

'Because I'm not trying to trap you into marriage? Never fear. You're quite safe from me.'

Was he safe? he wondered. Despite the circumstances, and the fact that she wasn't beautiful, he found her fascinating. She was intriguingly clever and her sharp humour appealed to him.

But more than that was the intense emotion that seemed to reach out from her in a way he couldn't understand. They never spoke of it. There was just a feeling that their mysterious closeness was inevitable, and that it was bound to grow.

The thought made him cautious. Developing warmer feelings for her would put him in her power, and that was something he always strove to avoid.

As the son of a count, he was used to young women pursuing him for the sake of his title. He'd thought himself well protected until the girl who'd once won his heart had betrayed him with the son of a duke. He would never forget the moment he'd discovered them in bed together—or the look she'd bestowed upon him, as though she despised him for daring to hope for her.

That had been several years ago, but the memory stayed with him. Love was unsafe. It caused danger and pain, and a wise man kept his distance.

But life without love did not mean life without marriage. One day he would have to take wife for the sake of producing an heir. His father had spoken of it in the last moments of his life.

'Marisa,' he'd murmured. 'She's perfect for you.'

Marisa was the daughter of a *barone* and an ideal choice for Vittorio's wife—at least according to his father. For a year he'd made his wishes plain. But Vittorio had resisted. He was on good terms with Marisa, but only in a brotherly way. Despite her youth and beauty, she did not attract him. Nor did he want a wife he hadn't chosen for himself.

When he returned to Rome he knew that Marisa and various similar problems would be waiting. But with Jackie's friendship to support him he felt more at ease.

The taxi was waiting to take them to the airport.

'You'll like Rome. Your Italian is good enough to help you feel at home.'

'Do you spend a lot of time in the city?'

'Yes—plenty.'

'But isn't your time taken up with managing your estates?'

'I have to do that as well, of course, but I have an estate manager who handles the difficult stuff. Mostly my time is taken up with the department store.'

'You actually *work* there?'

'Does that surprise you? You think I'm useless

for anything except lying around enjoying my title while others do the work?'

'After the way you've rescued me I'm not likely to think you useless.'

He gave her a teasing glance. 'Very tactfully said.'

'Yes, I've got to stay on your right side, haven't I? Why don't you tell me some more about the store so that I can flatter you further?'

'It sells a wide range of goods which I buy from all over the world. You're going to be very valuable to the business. But I've already told you that.'

'Yes, you grabbed me because I could be useful. Sheer cynical self-interest. Just what a businessman needs. Well done.'

They shared a laugh.

'Glad to see you're a realist,' he said. 'Would it be insulting to suggest that you too have some cynical self-interest?'

'No, I'd take it as a compliment.'

'Good for you.'

'Working for you is going to teach me a whole lot of things that I can use in my future career.' She gave him a thumbs-up sign. 'Here's to cynical self-interest.'

'The most useful motive in the world,' he agreed, making the same gesture.

'Cheers!'

They shook hands.

At last the airport came into view. Soon they were queuing for their flight and boarding the plane.

Jackie was taken aback to discover that Vittorio had booked the most expensive first class seats. But then, why wouldn't he? He was a count and a successful businessman, wasn't he?

'Take the window seat,' he said. 'It's more interesting that way.'

'Is it a long flight?' she asked as the plane began to move slowly down the runway.

'Only two and a half hours.'

Never having flown before, she was nervous. But she managed to stay at ease until take-off, and then gazed out of the window as the ground fell away.

'What will happen when we get there?' she asked.

'We'll be met at the airport by my Aunt Tania. She lives with me and looks after the house. I called her this morning and asked her to prepare a room for you.'

Before she could reply, the plane quivered. She took a sharp, nervous breath and clenched her hands.

'It's all right,' Vittorio said. 'Planes always shake when they go through clouds. We're not going to crash.'

'No—I realise—it's just that—'

'It's just that you're afraid of flying.'

'I've never flown before.'

'Is there anything else bothering you?' he asked, regarding her with concern.

'Just a little headache. It's not too bad.'

He took her hand in his. 'Probably caused by nerves. Don't worry. We'll soon be there.'

CHAPTER FOUR

AT LAST THEY landed at Leonardo da Vinci Airport. They spent a few minutes collecting their bags and then they were able to make their way out. Jackie looked around, trying to come to terms with what was happening.

'Ah, there she is,' Vittorio said suddenly.

He began waving into the distance at a middle-aged woman who was waving back to him. The woman began to run forward and he hastened towards her until they were in each other's arms. Jackie reckoned this must be the Aunt Tania he had mentioned.

She moved a little closer, waiting for him to introduce them. But then his aunt turned aside, revealing a young woman who ran forward and threw herself into Vittorio's arms.

Jackie could see that he was tense. He embraced the girl formally, before standing back and turning to indicate Jackie. She couldn't make out exactly what he was saying, but she gathered it wasn't revealing.

'This is my Aunt Tania,' he told Jackie. 'And my friend Marisa. I've told them that we are planning a business arrangement that has made it necessary for you to see Rome.'

'Welcome to our city,' Aunt Tania said politely. 'Vittorio says you will be staying with us. That will be lovely.'

'Did you give her the best guest room?' Vittorio asked.

'Yes, just as you said. Now, let's go home.'

'Have you got a taxi waiting?'.

'No, Marisa drove me here.'

'And I can drive you home,' Marisa said quickly. 'This way.'

When they reached her car she pulled open the door next to the front passenger seat, indicating for Vittorio to get in beside her. He did so, leaving Jackie and Tania to sit together in the back.

It was a lengthy journey out of the city and through the countryside to the Martelli estate. Jackie studied the scenery, occasionally looking round to find Vittorio's aunt regarding her with curiosity.

'So you're here on business,' Tania said. 'What kind of business are you in?'

She took a sharp breath, caught off-guard, and felt troubled about how to answer.

Vittorio came to her rescue.

'Jackie's a specialist in merchandising,' he said, glancing back over his shoulder. 'What she doesn't know about display and point of sale isn't worth knowing.'

Jackie suppressed an ironic smile at his way of describing her work behind the counter in a little shop.

'So you're going to help my nephew run his business?' Tania queried.

'If I can. And I hope he can teach me something that will be useful,' she said.

To her relief, the subject was allowed to drop. Soon they reached the estate and the car swept through extensive grounds up to a great house.

'We're nearly there,' Vittorio said, pointing out of the car window. 'A little further and you'll see my home.'

As he spoke a large building came into view. Jackie gasped at its elegance and beauty.

'My goodness, it's like a palace!' she gasped.

'My ancestors had rather grandiose ideas. It

was a matter of pride for them to live in a splendid home.'

And I bet it took a lot of money to maintain, she thought, forcing some of them into acts of dishonesty.

Perhaps the same thought had occurred to Vittorio, for he fell silent then.

'We only live in small part of it now,' Tania said. 'But we still relish the rest, which has a marvellous history.'

A woman whom Jackie took to be the housekeeper was waiting for them as they left the car and climbed the steps to the front door. Vittorio took the bags.

'I'll take these up to Jackie's room,' he said. 'Come along, Jackie.'

Inside, the building was just as luxurious. In a daze she followed him up the stairs and along a corridor until they reached her room. Like the rest of the house it was luxuriously appointed. A large bed took up most of the space, and the walls were lined with elegant wardrobes.

'The maid will be here to help you unpack,' he said. 'Are you all right? You look as though something's the matter.'

'I'm just confused. I can't get my head around

everything that's happening. I've never been anywhere like this before.'

'Don't worry—you'll soon feel at home. I'll
see to that.'

The words were kindly spoken, but it flashed
across her mind that she could never feel at home
in this place, surrounded by a luxury that haunted
her with memories of her father's impoverished
home.

Marisa appeared in the doorway, followed by
a maid.

'This is Gina,' she said. 'She speaks English
and she will help you.'

Vittorio patted her shoulder. 'I'll leave you to
unpack now and I'll see you at supper.'

He followed Marisa out of the room.

Gina immediately got to work, unpacking the
bags and putting things away.

Jackie watched her, trying to believe what was
happening.

'Here you have a little bathroom,' Gina said.
'And through these windows you have a wonderful view.'

It was true. She was only one floor up, but
looking out onto lawns that soon vanished into

trees. The sun was setting, casting a glow ever everything.

'No, no, no!'

The cry from a female voice streamed upwards from below. Leaning out, Jackie was unable to see anyone, but she could tell the sound had come from behind a wall.

'Marisa—'

That was Vittorio. But after that one word he got no further for Marisa exploded again.

'Perche, Vittorio? *Perche?'*

Marisa was talking too fast for Jackie to understand much, but she knew that *perche* meant *why.* It was clear that Marisa was demanding an explanation and Vittorio was trying to make her be quiet.

Jackie recalled the suspicious glances Marisa had given her. Plainly her arrival was unwelcome.

The sound died and she turned back to the room. Gina was a skilled maid with a shrewd eye. She studied Jackie's appearance before casting her glance over several of the clothes.

'You are lucky, *signorina,'* she said. 'You have a slim figure. That is a blessing.'

'Slim?' Jackie brooded. 'That's one way of putting it. In England I've been called skinny—even scrawny.'

'*Scusami, signorina*. Scrawny?'

'In English it's a way of telling someone they're too thin.'

'No, no,' Gina protested passionately. 'You cannot be too thin for fashion. Rome is a city of great fashion. Everything will be fine for you here—especially when you've bought some new clothes.'

'Oh—well—I don't think I'll be buying new clothes,' Jackie said uneasily.

The maid's words were like a blow, reminding her how little cash she had.

'But you *must*. Everyone will want to meet you.'

'That's true,' said Vittorio from the doorway.

How long had he been standing there? Jackie wondered. How much had he seen and heard?

'My new business associate will make quite an entrance,' he said.

With a slight gesture of his head he dismissed Gina, who left the room.

'New clothes,' he said. 'You do need them. We can make arrangements tomorrow.'

'But I can't. I haven't got any money to buy clothes.'

'You crazy woman! I offered you a million pounds and you chucked it back in my face. Now you're complaining about poverty.'

'I'm not complaining,' she said defiantly. 'I'm being practical.'

'So be practical and accept my offer.'

'*No!* Not that. You don't understand, do you?'

'No—and I don't think you understand your own actions.'

He was wrong, she thought. She completely understood the reasons for her stubborn refusal to yield.

If she accepted the money he would consider the debt settled. And that idea was agony to her. For the sake of her father's memory she would never allow him to do that—however much she might need the money.

'Oh, you really *are* contrary, woman,' he growled.

'What's that supposed to mean?'

'You've hardly got a penny to your name but you turn down the best financial offer you'll ever have and treat me as a villain for making it. That's carrying illogicality to new heights.'

'Not illogicality. Pride. Memory of my father's suffering.'

'You think your father would want you to refuse?'

'Yes, because accepting would be like saying what happened to him doesn't matter.'

'I think he loved you too much for that. I think he'd have been glad to see things get better for you.'

'You— How dare you speak of him like that?'

'I only said he loved you. Didn't he?'

'Yes—with all his heart. But you have no right to make use of him like that.'

'All right, I'll say no more. But think about it, Jackie. What sort of future would he have wanted for you? Prosperous? Or living on the edge of poverty? If he was here now, listening to us, what do you think he'd say to you? *Take every penny and live well.* Or, *Tell him to keep his money and get stuffed. Give yourself the pleasure of kicking him in the teeth. Then live on the edge of poverty.*'

'Stop it!' she cried, backing away from him, hands over her ears. *'Stop it!'*

He reached out and for a moment she thought he would take hold of her. But then he dropped his hand, moving quickly away.

'I'll see you at supper,' he said, and left without another word.

As he closed the door she struggled with the desire to hurl something at it. It was shocking for him to put words into her father's mouth just to suit himself. But there was no doubt that he *was* baffled by her refusal to take his money, and she reckoned the reason was plain. A man so wealthy was used to being able to buy whatever he wanted.

Not just wealthy, she mused. He was handsome also. *Too* handsome. He must be used to women collapsing at his feet and promising to do anything he wanted.

But not me, Vittorio. You've met the one woman who'll gladly tell you exactly where to go.

She wondered if she'd been wise to come here when their hostility was still acute. But he'd saved her from Rik. She would just have to cope as best she could.

To distract herself, she began going through her possessions.

She soon realised that Gina had put her finger on an unexpected problem when she'd spoken of Rome as being a city of great fashion. None of her clothes were fashionable. At best they might be described as serviceable, with several pairs of jeans and dresses that were plain.

Hurriedly she went through the clothes and found something that might do for the evening meal. It was pale grey, neat and slightly elegant. A few moments in front of the mirror gave her a chance to work on her hair, but she wasn't pleased with the result. Drawn back tightly it merely looked dreary. Left to fall around her face it seemed neglected.

There was a knock at the door and Gina appeared.

'Ah, *signorina*, I know what I can do for you. It will soon be time for supper, so I will take care of your hair.'

She had come prepared with hair tongs, and Jackie watched in awe as Gina turned her severe locks into a bundle of delightful curls.

'Thank you,' she said with feeling. 'It's so nice of you to take so much trouble for me.'

'Signor Vittorio said I was to do everything you needed to help you be at your best. He wants you to be happy.'

'How kind of him.'

Was he being kind, or did he just want to keep her quiet and uncomplaining? she wondered.

A moment later there came a knock on her door, and Vittorio entered.

'Excellent,' he said, regarding her. 'Our guests will be impressed.'

'Guests? Are there many coming?'

'Yes, we've had a few phone calls from friends who want to drop in. It's going to be quite a busy party. Shall we go?'

He held out his arm to her and she took it. Together they left the room and headed along the corridor to the top of the stairs. As they arrived she saw a little crowd gathered in the hall below. There were three middle-aged men and several young women. Most notable among them was Marisa, who stood looking up as they descended.

'Our guests are here already,' Vittorio observed.

When he began the introductions Jackie could hardly believe her ears. Every man seemed to have a title. She managed to pick up the words *duca, visconte, barone*... They exchanged greetings with them, their wives and their elegant young daughters.

Wow, she thought. Cinderella certainly had come to the ball tonight.

She wondered why they were all here. But

when she saw how she was being regarded by the younger women a suspicion came over her. It was no accident that they were here. Marisa had clearly spread the word of her arrival, alarming all those who aimed to be the next Contessa.

'Let's go and have something to eat,' Tania said, leading the way into the dining room.

A long table dominated the centre of the room, with twenty places laid out. Vittorio escorted Jackie to a chair and sat beside her. She had the impression there was a faint disagreement on his other side, as two young women sought the chair beside him. But it was over in a moment.

The other seat beside Jackie was occupied by Aunt Tania, who was clearly still regarding her with interest. She had a thin, sharp face, which had a disconcerting habit of flashing into a brilliant smile.

'You must tell me all about yourself,' she said now. 'I'd never heard of you until Vittorio called me this morning to say he was bringing you. You're obviously a very significant business associate.'

'I'm afraid he makes me sound too important.'

'Jackie is too modest about her abilities,' Vittorio said. 'When I expand my English business in Rome I'll be doing everything she says.'

Tania raised her coffee cup in salute.

'Congratulations, *signorina*. If you knew how rarely he follows anyone else's advice—or even listens to it—you'd realise what a unique position you hold. Believe me, I'll do all I can to make you feel welcome here.' She smiled. 'My nephew would be very annoyed with me if I didn't.'

'Of course. I'm here to help him make a profit. That's what really matters.'

The two women shared a laugh. Vittorio noticed and nodded with pleasure.

Servants appeared with the supper. Between the excellent food and the friendly talk Jackie had an enjoyable evening.

At last the younger women began to leave the table and settle on sofas. Two of them seized Vittorio and playfully forced him to join them. He was immediately surrounded by admirers.

'I look forward to showing you our house,' Tania said. 'There has been much history here— many notable people. Sometimes we have even opened it to tourists.'

'That sound fascinating,' Jackie said. 'I love history. In England I used to like visiting great historical buildings where dramatic things had happened in the past.'

'Then you'll enjoy Castello Martelli. We've had our fair share of excitement there.'

'Lovely. I even—'

She was checked by a shriek of laughter that came from a nearby sofa.

Glancing over, she saw that Vittorio was deep in conversation with Marisa and the other young women who crowded round him. All of them were rocking with laughter.

'Some more wine?' Tania asked.

'No, thank you,' Jackie said. 'Would you mind if I went to bed? It's been a long day. It was my first flight and it's left me a bit shaken.'

'Yes. It can take it out of you, can't it? Especially if you're nervous.'

'That's very true.'

'You look as if you've got a headache. Go to bed now. I'll send Gina up with something to drink.'

'Thank you.'

At the door Jackie looked back to wave goodnight to Vittorio, but he was still enjoying himself with his female companions, managing to be enfolded in three pairs of arms at once. He seemed to have forgotten that she existed.

As she watched Marisa intervened, pulling the others away but doing it with laughter, as though claiming Vittorio as her property was no more than a joke to her.

Vittorio looked up, noticed Jackie in the doorway and waved. She gave him a slight wave back and departed.

As promised, Gina brought something up to her room.

'English tea,' she said. 'My mistress said you were to have the best.'

'She's being very kind to me.'

'She likes you. She doesn't like that other one, but if the Count marries her—well, what can we do? Goodnight, *signorina*.'

Gina slipped away, leaving Jackie to brood. And there was a great deal to brood about. However she had thought this visit would work out, it was happening very differently, and somehow she would need to find a way to deal with it.

She tensed suddenly, alerted by a noise from the corridor outside. There was the sound of a door being opened, and then Marisa's voice.

'Perché non si può solo ascoltare me?'

Jackie just managed to make out the meaning.
'Why can't you just listen to me?'

Vittorio's reply was also in Italian, but his
meaning was blindingly clear. 'Because there's
no point. We talk too much and it gets us nowhere. *You* won't listen to what *I* say.'

'Because I don't believe you really mean it. Listen to your *heart*, Vittorio—'

'I *am* listening to it, and it's saying no. There's
nothing there. Goodbye, Marisa.'

Quietly Jackie looked out, just in time to see
Marisa storming away down the corridor as the
door opposite was closed.

So that was his room, she thought.

Glancing around to make sure Marisa was no
longer there, she went and knocked at his door.

He opened it at once. 'Marisa, *per favore*—
Oh, it's you.'

Looking shocked, he checked himself and drew
back to let her in.

'Yes, it's only me,' she said, following him. 'I
reckon it's time for you to come clean, Vittorio.
You've concealed the truth for long enough.'

'What truth? What are you talking about?'

'I mean the reason you brought me here. You
played the gallant knight, rescuing me from Rik,

but it was actually about Marisa, wasn't it? You wanted to stop her troubling you and I'm a handy excuse.'

Vittorio closed his eyes like a man wondering how to cope with another disaster.

'It's a bit more than that…' He groaned. 'It's not just Marisa.'

'So it's all the others who hunted you down today?'

'I don't think it's an accident that so many people—women—turned up. They came to see *you*.'

'You think they're all competing for *you*? I've heard of conceit, but that takes the biscuit.'

'You're wrong. I'm not vain enough to think girls are after me for myself. It's the title they want, and they're not the only ones. My father tried to arrange a marriage between myself and Marisa. I told him I wasn't keen, but he wouldn't listen. He was so certain he could persuade me that he let her think it was all arranged. She reckons I'm her property, and if I so much as look at another woman she acts like a betrayed wife. It's getting more than I can stand. Why do you think they came today? Marisa spread the word that I'd arrived with you and they all descended on us to get a look at you. So, yes, I thought your presence

here might help me, and I seized the chance because I'm going crazy with this situation.'

'But you didn't think to tell me?'

'I was going to but—well—I just lost my nerve.
Suppose I *had* told you? What would you have
done? Agreed to help me? I don't think so.'

'You're wrong. After the way you helped me
deal with Rik I'll do anything I can for you.'

His eyes gleamed. 'Anything?'

'Anything at all.'

'You'll help save me from Marisa?'

She smiled. 'I'll go into battle against her and
you'll be quite safe.'

'That would be wonderful. Just keeping her
thinking we're an item. It may just work.'

'But why does it have to be me? Why couldn't
you pick someone else?'

'Because you have one great advantage that
makes you a better choice than anyone else.'

'What could that possibly be?'

'You've made it plain you don't like me or trust
me. Another woman might take my attentions
seriously, think I meant them, and then be hurt
when she learned the truth. But *you* see me as a
cold and arrogant—mercenary, even. That's fine.
There's no danger that you'll ever fall in love with

me. I know we've decided to be friends, but it's a cautious friendship with suspicion on both sides, and that makes us both safe.'

She regarded him ironically.

'So you chose me because you knew I'd never embarrass you by indulging in romantic thoughts about you? Oh, were you right about that!'

'That's what I reckoned. You'd sooner swoon over a slimy octopus than me.'

'I wouldn't go so far as to say *that*.'

'But you were thinking it?'

She regarded him with her head on one side. 'Maybe. Sometimes it's best to keep your thoughts to yourself. I'm sure you know all about that.'

'It's been useful. Let's shake on it.'

They clasped hands.

'Your aunt doesn't like Marisa, does she?' she observed.

'No, but she's my father's sister, and as such she feels bound by his wishes.'

'Nonsense. The only wishes that matter are yours.'

His face brightened. '*That's* what I like to hear a woman say.'

'Aha! You think it shows I have a submissive

nature? She rubbed her hands. 'I could have a nasty shock waiting for you.'

'I'm sure you will. And I'm equally sure it will be interesting.'

From outside the building came the sound of voices. Vittorio opened the window and looked down.

'They're leaving,' he said. 'Come here.'

She went to stand beside him and he put his arm around her. Down below, Marisa was approaching her car while the other guests streamed out around her. Suddenly Marisa turned her head, gazing up at them.

'Shall we try to convince her now?' Vittorio murmured.

'Yes—what shall we do?'

'Rest your head on my shoulder.'

She did so, and he tightened his arm about her.

'Look up at me,' he murmured.

As soon as she did he leaned down and kissed her forehead.

Jackie drew a slow breath, waiting for him to drift lower until his lips touched hers. But he stayed as he was.

'She's there…watching us,' he said. Let's make this look good.'

His arms tightened, drawing her closer. His free hand caressed her cheek before drifting down, briefly touching her breasts. Jackie trembled, longing fiercely to take things further.

'You said you wanted me to help you...' she whispered.

'Yes—what are you going to do?'

'This,' she said, and reached up so that her arms went around his neck, drawing his head down so that she could caress his mouth with her own.

She could sense the surprise that shook him, then felt his grip on her tighten as he took control, moving his mouth against hers with growing urgency.

Caution told her that she shouldn't do this, but she couldn't make herself be cautious. Desire stormed through her, destroying everything but the need to be his and make him hers.

At last he spoke, his voice shaking. 'I think—I think we've done almost enough to convince her.'

'Yes—yes—'

'Just a few moments more...' His mouth brushed hers again.

Down below, Marisa got into her car. At the last moment she glanced up at them, made a sneering face, then started the car and drove away.

CHAPTER FIVE

'SHE'S GONE,' VITTORIO WHISPERED.

He could almost hear his own voice shaking. The last few minutes had affected him intensely, making him yearn to go further. But he struggled for control, fearful of driving Jackie away.

Reluctantly he released her. 'You did it. Marisa saw enough to get the message. Perhaps I should be grateful to you for taking command.'

'I didn't take command—'

'Didn't you?'

She thought she could guess his meaning. When she had reached up to draw his head down closer to hers, he'd known that her desire was as strong as his, and there was no way she could deny it. He had probably read the message in her eyes.

'You found the right way for both of us,' he said. 'You could say I followed your lead.'

'It was necessary for the performance,' she reminded him. 'Anything's worth doing for an effective performance.'

'Well said! A woman with efficient instincts.'

'And efficiency is everything,' she said lightly.

She met his gaze, both of them knowing that the real message was something quite different.

'Sometimes efficiency really *is* everything,' he said softly. 'But then—things change.'

'Well, they've changed for Marisa. I can't think why she's worried about me. I'm no beauty. And don't bother to give me a polite answer or I'll thump you.'

'Right. You're no beauty. I heartily agree,' he said, trying to sound casual. He met her eyes. 'But you do have something else that's more than looks. You've got wit, and an intelligence that I find most appealing. In fact, since the day we met you've caught me out and tripped me up more than anyone's ever done before.'

'Then I'm surprised you brought me here.'

'Yes, I wonder what I was thinking of. I guess I don't mind being caught at a disadvantage—every now and then.'

'I'll remember that. I could have fun tripping you up.'

'I bet you will. There are women who conquer

a man by their beauty, and those who conquer him by keeping him nervous, even scared.'

'And there's no doubt which one *I* am!' She laughed. 'But maybe I don't *want* to conquer you.'

'You won't make the effort? Then I'd feel insulted. Besides, you do it without meaning to.'

'You don't know that. I might have a fiendish plan going on.'

'I live in hope. But for the moment I'll say goodnight. We have a busy day tomorrow. You should beware. When we get to Rome I'm going to work you to death.'

'That's what I hoped. Anything else would be dull.'

'And let's not be *dull*, whatever we do.'

'No. Not that you could ever be dull here,' she murmured, glancing around at his bedroom. Like the rest of the house, it was lavishly decorated in a medieval style.

'This was my father's room,' he said.

'And now it's yours because you're the Count? Do you think you can be grandiose enough?'

'I'll try to be. I've never thought of myself as grandiose, but I suppose everything is going to be different now.'

'Yes,' she murmured. 'That's true. You won your battle tonight. Marisa saw us, which is exactly what you wanted. From now on you'll be a free man.'

'A free man?' He looked into her eyes. 'I wonder just what that means?'

She met his gaze, suddenly confused. 'You'll find out gradually. I'm here to help you.' A sudden impulse made her say. 'It's getting late and I'm tired. I think I'll go to bed now. Goodnight.'

'Goodnight. And, Jackie—thank you for everything.'

She smiled and fled. It had suddenly become vital to escape him quickly and take refuge in her room.

Once there, she paced the floor, trying to understand the conflicting thoughts and feelings that struggled for supremacy inside her head.

It was madness to be upset, she told herself. Vittorio was a man of good looks and charm. Any woman would be thrilled to be taken into his arms. And for a brief moment she had known that delicious excitement. To feel his lips caressing hers, sense the tremors in his body—those pleasures had consumed her. He had wanted her, and the blissful knowledge had driven her to a response that had been almost beyond her control.

But then, like a warning blast, a voice in her mind had warned her to take care. To guard her feelings. He'd embraced her in order to deceive Marisa, then released her when Marisa had no longer been able to see them.

He was only pretending, she thought. He'd pretend for just long enough to get what he wanted and then she'd have outlived her usefulness to him. Just as if she fell in love with him he'd find it useful. And that was all he wanted of her—to be useful. Useful in the department store, useful about the money problem, useful about Marisa.

She'd do well to remember that falling for Vittorio would be extremely hazardous to her health. Mind you, he'd be as a big a fool to fall for *her*!

With Jackie gone Vittorio stood without moving for some moments, trying to cope with conflicting feelings. This had been his father's bedroom, and it still contained many memories.

Here they had spent their last few moments together, and Franco had revealed the secret that had set Vittorio on a new path. Putting right his father's wrongs had seemed like the right thing to do—and a simple thing.

But before that there had been other talks. Some of them about Vittorio's mother. He knew that both his parents had been unfaithful in their brief marriage. Adele, his mother, had married for the title—something which Franco, deeply in love, had not suspected until it was too late.

Looking at the surroundings where his father had made his last confession, he found that another scene came back to him. Then, too, Franco had lain there, dizzy with suffering, driving himself to tell the painful truth to his son, who had knelt beside the bed.

'I lost track of all the men she had...' He'd sighed.

Filled with fear, Vittorio had asked quickly, 'Do you mean that I'm not your son?'

'No, you're mine. When you were born I had a DNA test done to check, and the result was all I had hoped. But the fact that such a test was needed—' He had given a deep groan before adding wretchedly, 'And the other child...'

'What other child?'

'Do you remember how we lost your mother when you were twelve? She died giving birth.

The baby also died. It wasn't mine. We hadn't made love for a long time, so I knew. She had never loved me as I loved her. I would have forgiven her, because I so much wanted her to stay with me, but then she was gone.'

'But how could you have kept her with you, knowing what you knew?' Vittorio had asked desperately.

'Yes, it's madness, isn't it? But love *is* a kind of madness. When you love a woman so much that you'll forgive her anything as long as she doesn't leave you, it's as though you cease to be yourself. I should have divorced her years before. I'd have been safer without her there to torment me. But I couldn't do it. I told myself I stayed with her for your sake, because you needed a mother. But the truth was I couldn't bear to let her go. So we stayed together…she kept living her riotous life. And then she died.'

Vittorio hadn't been able to reply. He'd dropped his head down into the bed, close to his father's, feeling only despair.

Franco had touched him. 'I pray that your life may be filled with more hope,' he'd said. 'Don't give your love to a woman who deceives you. Be cautious, my son. Don't trust too easily. Keep your love to yourself as long as you can.'

The advice had touched Vittorio's heart. Only recently he'd quarrelled with a young woman who'd briefly inspired his trust and affection before turning to another man. Everything in him had accepted that his father had been right, and that he must be cautious.

But then he'd met Jackie—frank, honest, different from any other women he'd met. Or so he'd thought until his growing attraction to her had begun to alarm him. Holding her in his arms, he'd felt a surge of feeling that was not merely desire, but also tenderness. And the awareness of her trembling in his arms, the fervour with which she'd kissed him, had left him feeling stunned.

She'd called it efficiency, claiming to have done no more than follow his lead. But the memory of her response lingered…delightful, alarming, warning him that the road ahead led into mystery.

It was unbearable not to know the answer. He went out into the corridor, looking to see if there was a light under her door. But there was none. Had she really gone to sleep? Or was she lying in the darkness, facing a confusion as great as his own?

He stood outside her door, listening to the silence inside, trying to decide whether to call her or knock. But after hesitating a long time he backed away, sensing that this was not the right moment.

Next morning Jackie awoke early and took a shower. Standing under the water, she wondered what she would see in Vittorio's eyes this morning. She'd felt sure he would call on her the previous night, but nothing had happened.

She'd heard a faint sound, as though his footsteps had approached her room, but then there had been only silence. Unable to bear the tension, she'd leapt out of bed and pulled open her door. But the corridor outside had been dark and empty, with no sign of him. She had gone back to bed and lain there fretting until she'd managed to fall asleep.

This morning her thoughts were still troubled—even more so because her attraction towards Vittorio made her feel that she was failing her father again.

Somehow, somewhere, there must be a way to do the right thing. If only she could find it.

She dressed and went downstairs into the hall.

Through an open door she could see Vittorio sitting at a desk.

He glanced up and waved to her. 'We'll be going in to breakfast in a moment,' he said. 'And then we can—'

The sound of the phone interrupted him, making him curse slightly and then answer it. Jackie went to stand by the window, gazing out at the grass and trees, entranced by their beauty. Clearly it was a magnificent estate, and she was curious to see more of it.

Glancing around, she saw that he had his back to her, absorbed in the call. Yielding to temptation, she slipped out of the door into the garden. For a few moments it was delightful to run across the lawn to where she could see a seat under one of the trees. She sat down on it and leaned back, closing her eyes and breathing in the cool air.

When at last she opened her eyes she found herself gazing at the building that reared up so magnificently, beautiful and luxurious. But the sight caused sorrow to fall over her heart, as it had done so often since she'd arrived here. This had been the home of the man who had cheated her beloved father, reducing him to poverty and despair.

In her mind's eye she saw her father again, his head sunk in misery when his wife had left him.

He had nothing, she thought. *And the man who lives here has everything.*

She could feel tears pouring down her cheeks and ducked her head, seizing a handkerchief to wipe them away. But there were more tears, followed by sobs. She sat there shaking, trying vainly to control her grief.

'Jackie— *Jackie?*'

The voice from overhead made her look up to see Vittorio standing there. At once he sat down beside her, reaching out to her.

'Come here,' he said.

'No!' She pulled sharply away. 'Go away. Leave me alone.'

'But I—'

'I said leave me alone. I don't want to talk to you.'

She jumped up, fleeing away from him until she plunged into the trees. When she felt safely out of sight she leaned against a tree trunk and abandoned the effort to control her tears.

Suddenly she felt a pair of strong arms go around her, pulling her against him.

'I'm sorry,' he said. 'I don't mean to crowd you, but stay with me a while. Let me help you.'

She couldn't answer. The feel of his chest was warm and comforting, giving her a pleasure she hadn't thought to know. She trembled and felt him draw her even closer.

'Cry,' he said. 'You need to. Don't fight it.'

It felt incredible that she was letting this man, of all men, comfort her. But the feel of his arms about her was unlike anything that had ever happened to her before.

'Let's go inside,' he said. 'We'll have breakfast and then go into the city. We've got a lot to do.'

'Oh, yes,' she said wryly. 'I'm going to give you all that expert opinion—if I can think of anything. I really felt very awkward when you were telling your aunt how good I am.'

'You played your part beautifully.'

'But I don't even know what I'm supposed to be expert *about*.'

'That's why we're going into town. By the time we've finished you'll be able to give me your orders.'

She rubbed her hands. 'Roll on the day!'

'Well, I've been meaning to tell you—' He stopped, realising that he no longer had her attention. She was looking about her at the medieval beauty of her surroundings as though something had suddenly struck her, 'What's the matter?' he asked.

'Nothing. It's this place,' she said. 'I just have to keep looking at it. It's wonderful how history seems to live here all around us, as though your ancestors were still alive.'

'I know the feeling. I've felt them with me all my life, and if I want to meet them I go to the gallery, where their portraits hang. Would you like to see it?'

'I'd love to.'

He led her into a great room at the back of the house. Portraits hung all along the walls, of people dressed in clothes that spoke of past centuries.

'And *all* these are your ancestors?' Jackie mused in wonder.

'Not all. Have a look at this one.'

He drew her to a full-length picture showing a young woman in a horse-drawn chariot. With one hand she controlled the horses, in the other she held a sword. On her head she wore a military helmet.

'That's Bellona,' Vittorio told her. 'The Roman goddess of war.'

'You have a *female* deity of war? Surely—?'

'Surely it should be a man?' he said, grinning. 'In any other society it probably would be. But in Rome we like strong, powerful women.'

'Unless they happen to disagree with you?' she teased, her eyes challenging him.

'Ah, well, let's not go into that.'

'Very wise,' she said with mock solemnity. 'Just think of all the awkward things I could remind you of.'

'And how you'd enjoy doing it.'

Tania had slipped into the room behind them and was listening to them with pleasure.

'You'll have a chance to meet Bellona,' she said. 'We celebrate her festival every year. You'll probably enjoy that.'

'Yes, you two have a lot in common...' Vittorio observed.

'Vittorio!' Tania protested. 'I hope you're not being rude to our guest.'

'Don't worry, Aunt. Jackie's not offended. And here's someone else you should meet,' Vittorio said, turning her towards a picture of a man in a suit of armour. 'He was the very first Count Martelli. And the two men in the next picture are his sons. The elder one died and the younger one inherited the title.'

Along the walls they went, with Vittorio describing his ancestors one by one, introducing them as though they still lived with him.

One portrait especially seized Jackie's attention. It showed a man in the luscious garb of the seventeenth century, with long curling hair falling over his shoulders. But it was his face that claimed her attention. It was Vittorio's face that had come down the centuries.

'He was my great-great-great-great-grandfather,' Vittorio said.

'Yes, I can see. It's incredible. You're really one of them. Hey—what's that?'

Her attention had been seized by another picture, a few feet along. It showed two men dressed in the attire of ancient Rome. One of them also had a face similar to Vittorio's.

'He must be another ancestor of yours,' she said. 'Who's the man with him?'

'Julius Caesar—the Roman Emperor.'

'One of your family was a friend of *Julius Caesar*? They even had their portraits painted together?'

'Not at all. There's a common belief that one

of my ancestors was part of Caesar's court, but
that picture was painted hundreds of years later.
It's just a fantasy. There are several fantasies like
that in this gallery. Over here is Napoleon. When
he was Emperor of France he annexed Rome, but
when he was defeated we regained our freedom.'

The picture had been carefully designed to
show Napoleon regarding his companion with
admiration and respect. The companion's face
also bore a notable resemblance to Vittorio's.

'It's marvellous, isn't it?' said Tania.

'That face—it's *him*!' Jackie exclaimed in wonder.

'Yes, you can't get away from me even a few
hundred years later.' Vittorio laughed.

'Have you shown Jackie the picture of Lady
Nanetta?' Tania asked.

'Not yet, but I'm looking forward to doing it.'
He guided her across the room. 'Nanetta is a family legend,' he explained. 'She was a magnificent
woman, but also an alarming one.'

He paused before a full-length picture of a tall,
slender woman.

'She had dozens of suitors,' he said, 'but she
rejected them all. Legend says that she was a

witch. It's never been proved or disproved, but she inspired a lot of fear.'

'Why did she reject them all?' Jackie asked. 'Didn't she ever fall in love?'

'Never. She had a great fortune and she believed that was all men wanted of her. She said no man could be trusted, nor was ever worthy of love.'

'How sad to believe that,' Jackie murmured. 'How could anyone endure life with nothing to believe in?'

'Is love the *only* thing to believe in?' he asked wryly.

'Of course there's always money.'

'But you don't believe in that, having turned down so much.'

'If you mean your million pounds, I turned it down for love—of my father.' She saw tension come into his face and added, 'There's more than one kind of love.'

He hesitated before saying, 'You're right, of course.'

She went to stand before the woman's picture, trying to see if her face revealed anything. But Lady Nanetta stared into the distance, concealing her secrets.

'I wonder what taught her so much distrust?' Jackie said.

'She saw a lot of evidence to distrust in her life. She was hugely rich.'

'Which was why so many men wanted to marry her?'

'Probably. Of course they may have been attracted to her as well.'

'I doubt that,' Jackie said, studying the picture. 'She was no beauty.'

Vittorio considered the picture before glancing back at her. 'That matters little,' he said. 'A woman doesn't have to be a great beauty to intrigue men. Her moods, her wit, the hint of mystery she can carry—those can lure men as keenly as mere good looks.' After a thoughtful moment he added, 'Sometimes more so.'

He was giving her a look that might have been significant. She tried to be cautious about understanding it, but there was a glint in his eye she couldn't ignore.

She called common sense to her rescue. 'If you say so,' she said cheerfully.

'I *do* say so.'

'Then I'll have to believe it—however unconvincing.'

He chuckled and put his arm around her. 'Let's get going—we have a busy day ahead of us,' said Vittorio. 'But first we'll have breakfast.'

They ate quickly, and when breakfast was over he led Jackie out of the palace to a garage around the side. He regarded her curiously as she took out her purse and examined its contents.

'Need some money?' he asked.

'No. Thank you, but I'm quite independent. I can use my bank card to draw money from my English account, can't I?'

'If you've got the pin number, yes.'

In a few moments they were on their way to Rome.

'What are we going to see first?' she asked.

'My department store. I need to see how it's managing. And I'll be interested in your opinion. After that, I'd like to show you some of the city.'

At first the road wound through the estate, and Jackie watched from the window, charmed by the green fields and forests, until finally the estate was behind them and they were heading along the motorway that led to the city.

Once in Rome, Vittorio drove straight to an area where there were shops, restaurants and commercial buildings. He parked the car and led her through the streets, letting her absorb the atmosphere until it was time to visit his department store.

It was a huge place, selling goods from many different countries and a vast range of sources. There were departments for furniture, glass, hardware and jewellery.

Jackie walked through it in a daze of delight. Everywhere Vittorio introduced her to the staff as 'my expert from England'. In the glass and china department he explained that she was to be in charge, and she was treated with great respect.

When he was called away for a moment the staff crowded round her, full of eager questions. Their English was efficient, as was her Italian.

'There are some products I'd like to show you,' she said. 'I'll need a computer.'

One was immediately made available, and she went online to show them the many sites where she found products that made them exclaim with admiration. It was clear that her visit was a success.

At last she looked up to find Vittorio regarding her with amused satisfaction.

'Found me any new stock?' he asked.

'One or two things I think might go well.'

She indicated several choices. He nodded in agreement to all of them, and a staff member began making purchases.

'We'll leave him to it while we look around some more,' Vittorio said. When they were outside he said, 'I wish you could have seen your face while you were giving everyone instructions. I think that's your idea of heaven.'

'If you mean that I'm a bully—'

'Only the kind of bully that I need working for me,' he said with a grin. 'You promised to make profit for me, and I can see that you will. Well done!'

'Thank you. After all, you did promise me authority.'

'I must have known by instinct that authority is your default position.'

'You might have a point there,' she said with a brief laugh. 'I must admit I *do* enjoy being the one to give the orders.'

'After the way you had to put up with Rik, I'm not surprised.'

'Not just Rik. I used to annoy my father a lot by arguing.' She regarded him cheekily. 'I'm a very difficult character.'

'Well, I already knew *that*.' He took her hand

in his and gave it a comforting squeeze. 'I can put up with you if you can put up with me.'

She squeezed back. 'I'll do my best—however hard it is.'

'I've got a feeling we're going to be a big success.'

Coming to Italy was proving to be everything she had dared to hope, thought Jackie. Here there were opportunities and a chance for the kind of new, more adventurous life that had once seemed impossible.

Suddenly she stopped.

'I didn't realise that your store stocked clothes.'

'Of course—it's our most popular department. Come and look.'

Jackie was soon in heaven! Vittorio introduced her to the staff and she watched, entranced, as boxes were opened to reveal costly gowns. She examined them, trying to imagine her dull self in any of the exquisite dresses.

'Perhaps—' she began, turning to Vittorio. 'Oh, where's he gone?'

'He was summoned to his office,' said Donna, the head assistant. 'Do you like our stock?

'Oh, yes, it's all so beautiful. Especially this

one.' She gazed admiringly at a black satin evening gown.

'Yes, it's one of our new range. Would you like to try it on?'

'I'm not sure… It looks very sophisticated, and I'm not really like that.'

'But you might be if you saw yourself in it.'

'Oh, go on, then—let's try.'

Donna's advice was good. The dress was tight-fitting, and clung perfectly to Jackie's slender figure, giving it a drama and mystery she'd never been aware of before.

She turned back and forth, enjoying the sight of her new self in the mirror. Totally absorbed, she failed to notice the middle-aged woman who had arrived, and was watching her with pleasure.

'Is that dress for sale?' the woman asked Donna.

'Yes, Contessa. It's part of the stock that's just arrived.'

'It would suit my daughter perfectly. I'll buy it.' The shopper turned to the man who had just appeared beside her. 'You're really extending your talents in this store. Doesn't your model look lovely?'

'Yes,' Vittorio murmured, 'she does.'

He backed away quickly before Jackie could

notice him. After a moment the Countess joined him. She was beaming.

'Now you have a satisfied customer,' she said. 'That dress looked so good on your model that I just *had* to buy it. Donna says it can be delivered tomorrow.'

He replied politely and escorted her away, before returning to the dress department. Jackie was still there, once more in her own clothes. For a moment Vittorio had a dizzying sensation that briefly she had become a different Jackie.

'It's time to move on, Jackie. We have a lot to fit in today.'

'Oh, that's a shame. I've had an amazing morning, and your store is magnificent.'

'No, no,' he said quickly. 'You mustn't say that. You're going to tell me how to bring it up to standard.'

'Suppose I think I can't?'

'Hush, don't say such a thing. Never admit failure.' He gave her a cheeky grin. 'You're here as an expert, giving me your lofty advice.'

'And you'll *take* my advice? I don't think so.'

'Then you can call me some suitable names. *Stupido, idiota, buffone.* You understand Italian well enough to take your pick.'

'I'll try to remember. Where to next, then?'

'I'd like to take you to my other shop. This one is much smaller. It could do with expansion, and I'd value your opinion.'

CHAPTER SIX

A SHORT STROLL brought them to the 'other shop', which she examined with interest, making notes. She was enjoying herself.

After a couple of hours they left.

Wherever they went Vittorio was instantly recognised. Even in the street people addressed him respectfully as 'Signor Conte', and regarded her with curiosity.

She could guess why she fascinated them. Word of her arrival had obviously spread fast, and she was clearly being regarded as the latest candidate for the position of Countess.

Me, she thought hilariously. *Plain, dreary me. Whatever next?*

'What's so funny?' Vittorio asked.

'Sorry—what?'

'You suddenly started laughing. People don't usually find Rome funny.'

'It's not Rome that's funny. It's me. Haven't you seen the way everybody is staring at me?'

'Sure—you've really got their attention.'

'And why? For the same reason Marisa is troubled by me. I'm seen as the latest candidate for your hand.'

'And that's funny, is it?'

'It is from the proper angle. Look.'

She pointed him towards the window of a shop they were passing. Turning, they looked at their reflections: Vittorio splendidly handsome, herself ordinary.

'Ever since the moment I came here,' she said, 'I've felt like Cinderella arriving at the ball.'

'Really? Does that make me Prince Charming?'

'Prince Charming or Prince Charm*less*. It depends on your mood.'

'You don't pull your punches, do you? Are you trying to lure me in or put me off?'

'What do *you* think?'

'I think you're trying to scare the life out of me. And succeeding.'

'That's all right, then. As long as you don't think I'm trying to lure you into marriage.'

'I promise never to think that.'

Vittorio wondered what he should have understood from her words. If she ever did set her sights on him he doubted he'd guess. She was too clever to be obvious. But the conversation had amused him too much to be troublesome.

'I'd better go into the bank while I'm here,' he said. 'The one across the road is the one I use.'

Inside the bank, she saw him treated with the same intense respect she had noticed before—which she guessed told her everything about the size of his bank balance.

'It would be easier if you banked here also, since you'll be living and working in Italy from now on,' he said. 'Tell them you want to transfer your London account.' He added lightly, 'Unless, of course, you're planning to dash back to the joys of working for Rik.'

'No chance!'

'Wise woman.'

He came to the counter with her and spoke in rapid Italian.

'There'll be bank cards for you in a couple of days,' he said at last. 'And now it's time for some lunch at last. This way.'

He led her to a little restaurant on the next corner.

As she looked through the menu he said, 'What would you like?'

'I don't know; I can't decide. I'll let you order for me.'

He regarded her with amused suspicion. 'You trust me to order for you? That's not like the Jackie I've come to know. Are you trying to catch me off-guard?'

'Well, I've got to do *something* to worry you, haven't I?'

'Don't bother. You worry me quite enough as it is.'

'In that case, please do your duty and order for me.'

He instructed the waitress, and in a few minutes a dish was set before her. It was a bowl filled with tiny lumps of meat and a few vegetables.

'It's called lamb *tagliata*,' he said. 'I remembered that you like lamb.'

'But that was the lunch we had in the hotel in London,' she said, astonished. 'You remembered from then?'

'Of course. I'm a businessman. I make efficient

notes about my business associates and use them
to my advantage.'

But he winked as he said it, and gave her a grin
which she returned.

The food tasted magnificent. She devoured it
with pleasure, aware that he was watching her
closely.

'Mmm…lovely,' she said. 'You choose food
well. I must put that in my own notes about *you*—
along with a few other things.'

He nodded, implying that he understood her
perfectly. 'Of course,' he said, 'my observations
will have to include how careless you are about
doing your job.'

'What?'

'You were supposed to be giving me an expert
opinion of my store. So far all you've done is eat.
I want to lodge a complaint.'

'I said it was magnificent!'

'But you were just being polite.'

'I'm *never* polite. Haven't you learned that yet?
Hmm… I'll have to give you a few lessons.'

'I'll look forward to it. But, in the meantime,
you didn't really *mean* magnificent, did you?'

'Suppose I say yes? Would that make me disappointing?'

'Come on, Jackie. Criticise. It's what you're here for.'

'Well, I *did* notice one thing missing. You have a huge range of things from all over the world, but I saw nothing from England.'

'That's because we've never had any real English expertise—until now. I did the right thing, kidnapping you.'

'You didn't exactly *kidnap* me,' she insisted. 'I wanted to come.'

'Suppose you hadn't? Do you think that would have made any difference?'

'No, I guess not.'

'You did a great job in the shop—especially when you modelled that dress.'

'Modelled—? You saw me?'

'Yes, I keep turning up when I'm not wanted, don't I? I was there with Contessa Valierse. She liked the sight of you so much she bought the dress for her daughter. I seem to gain from everything you do. As soon as I realised that, I decided that you must belong to me.'

'And if I resist?' she teased.

'It won't make any difference. When an efficient businessman finds something that suits him he takes possession of it, ignoring all distractions.'

'And you think nobody can successfully fight you?'

'That's right. I always get my own way. Make a special note of that.'

'Yes, I think I will.' She took out a scrap of paper, then discovered a problem.

'Damn! I haven't got a pen.'

'Here.' He handed her a pen.

'I wonder if I should accept that…' she mused.

'You mean because you're about to write something critical about me? Go on. Be brave.'

'Thanks.' She took it and scribbled, *He always gets his own way*, adding a little swirl afterwards.

'What's that squiggle at the end?' Vittorio asked.

'It's code. It means, *That's what he thinks.*' Jackie chuckled.

'Hmm… At least you're honest.'

'Well, I'm not sure you get your own way as much as you think you do.'

'You will be. In time.'

Despite the seemingly harsh words, the atmosphere was teasing and friendly.

'Of course it doesn't do for a guy to be too

self-confident around you,' he said. 'He'd pay a heavy price.'

'Or *I* would,' she said wryly.

He considered her. 'Is that the voice of experience?'

'There was a man I was once fond off. Just fond. His name was Peter. I wasn't passionately in love, but when he mentioned marriage I was interested.'

'What went wrong?'

'My father became ill. I was looking after him and Peter didn't like that. It made him feel that he came second.'

'*Did* he come second?'

'Yes, I suppose he did. He wanted me to put Daddy in a care home, but I couldn't do that. It would have broken his heart.'

'And Peter was angry about that?'

'We had a quarrel. I told him that he couldn't give me orders and that was that. In my admittedly limited experience I've discovered that men like to be in charge.'

'Surely that isn't aimed at *me*? You have as much control as I do.'

'Not as much. Maybe a bit.'

'We'll agree to disagree. So you sent him away with a flea in his ear?'

'Yes. He couldn't believe I meant it, but I wasn't going to change my mind. How about you? Have you never been tempted to settle down with any of the beautiful women who seem to throw themselves at you at any given opportunity?'

He made a face, but said nothing.

'I'm sorry,' she said. 'I didn't mean to pry. Your love life is none of my business.' She added cheekily, 'But perhaps you don't *have* one. Perhaps you live on a pinnacle of lofty indifference.'

'If only I did. There was one woman who taught me to be careful, and it was a strong lesson that I've never forgotten.'

'Was she after your title?'

'She was. But at first she played her role so convincingly that I didn't realise the truth. I was completely taken in—until the day I found her in bed with another man.'

'What? How *could* she?'

'The man was heir to a dukedom. His social standing and personal fortune were therefore much greater than my own. That told me everything I needed to know. Her fine words and loving behaviour towards me had been because she wanted my title. When a better title came along I ceased to exist as far as she was concerned.'

'She pretended to love you—?'

'It was a good act. Fooled me.'

'And you loved her?'

He hesitated, and she could tell that he found this hard to answer.

'I thought I did. But it was a useful lesson. I've never been deceived again. I keep my suspicious side working.'

His words were cool, but she had a sense that they concealed feelings he didn't want to admit. This deceitful woman had caused him a lot of pain—some of which had never completely abated.

'What a dreadful thing to happen,' she said. 'Can you ever trust anyone again?'

'Probably not. But it's safer that way. What about you? After this guy you sent away—has there been anyone since?'

'No, I've had too much to think about. First my father died, and after that I set my heart on saving up enough money to escape my miserable existence, start a new life.'

'But you could be doing that now, by taking the money I offered you. Why did you turn it down?'

'For Daddy's sake. It would have felt like insulting him—saying that his suffering didn't matter as long as I gained the money.'

'But he wouldn't know.'

'Maybe—maybe not. But I still value his opinion. What he would've thought about things is of paramount importance to me. What about you and *your* father's wishes? Don't you take *his* views into account when you make decisions? Isn't that what you were doing in trying to give me that money?'

Jackie was exactly right, he realised. His father was still there in his mind and his heart. At times it was as if he could hear his voice in his ear. And clearly the same was true of her. It was almost alarming.

'And do you feel that *he* would know whether you've managed it or not?' she asked.

'I don't know, of course,' he said quietly. 'But *I* will know.'

'And so will I. That's why I can't give in and take your money. I feel that it would break his heart.'

'And I have to keep my word to *my* father. If I don't, that would break *his* heart.'

'If only they could have talked to each other

while they were still alive,' she said wistfully. 'They could've sorted it out without us.'

He took her hand between his. 'Instead we must honour their memories and do right by them both.'

'Yes. I'm glad of that.'

He squeezed her hand. 'So am I.'

A waiter approached, making him release her quickly.

When he'd ordered some coffee he said, 'Let's discuss the store. You said it needed more stuff from England. Tell me exactly what you mean...'

After lunch they were soon in the car, heading back through the country to the Castello Martelli. As darkness fell she saw the building's lights from a distance, and marvelled again at its magnificence and beauty.

Tania was waiting in the hall.

'Shall I get you some supper?' she asked.

'No need—we've enjoyed a late lunch,' Vittorio told her cheerfully. 'And now we have something to celebrate. This way, Jackie.'

His arm around her waist, he guided her into his office. Tania regarded them wryly. After a moment she went to the office door and stood watching while Jackie worked on the computer, accessing one English website after another while showing Vittorio her ideas for supplying his stores.

'Can you go back to the last one?' Vittorio said. 'I like those metal ornaments. Yes, that's it. Zoom in on that one. Great. Yes, I'll have that.'

He became aware of Tania stood in the doorway.

'Come and look, Aunt. Jackie's doing a wonderful job for us.'

'So I see,' Tania said, coming forward, smiling. 'You really seem very knowledgeable, *signorina*.'

'Please call me Jackie.'

'Jackie. Yes. Now, if my nephew is going to work you to death can I get you some coffee—or tea? A glass of wine?'

'I'm okay—thank you, Tania.'

'I will take a wine, please, Aunt Tania,' said Vittorio.

The other woman smiled at them both and headed to the kitchen. Jackie sensed that Tania was still undecided about her, but her manner was pleasant.

Once Tania was gone, Jackie's attention was brought back to the computer screen.

'I want to go back to town tomorrow,' announced Vittorio, 'but tonight I want to see some of those websites again.'

'I'll get started now,' Jackie said.

He sat with his attention fixed on what she was doing. Suddenly he said, 'Let me look at that.'

She enlarged the picture, which was of a metal vase with elaborate engraving.

He studied it for several minutes before saying, 'Fine. I'll buy some of those.'

He purchased the items online, studied more websites and purchased several more things. By the time they were finished he'd spent a thousand euros and was in good spirits.

'Fantastic job!' he said. I'd never have found that stuff without you. And tomorrow there'll be more. We must make an early start.'

'Then I'll have an early night,' Jackie said, rising.

He rose too, but she signalled for him to sit down. Tania had just returned to the office with Vittorio's drink, and Jackie got the sense that she wanted to talk with her nephew privately.

Vittorio nodded, gave her a gentle kiss on the cheek, and let her go.

When they were alone Tania poured him a glass of wine. 'It's been a good evening,' she said.

'Yes. I knew bringing Jackie here would be brilliant. She really knows her stuff.'

'And she makes sure you realise it,' Tania observed lightly.

'You sound suspicious. I thought you liked her?'

'In a way, I do. That's what makes it confusing. I want to believe in her but—' She sighed.

'But what?'

'What exactly is she *after*?'

'Nothing.'

'Oh, my dear boy, be realistic. Every young woman you meet is after something. Usually money.'

'No, that's one thing I can be sure of. She's not after my money. I offered her money and she refused it.'

'Obviously it wasn't enough.'

'I offered her in excess of a million English pounds.'

'A million—? Are you out of your mind?'

'In a way, yes. I've been partly out of my mind since Papà admitted on his deathbed that he'd cheated Jackie's father out of a million years ago.'

Tania gasped. 'No, that's not possible. You've imagined it.'

'It's true. He told me he and George Benton both placed a bet. Benton's paid off, but Papà stole the winnings before Benton knew. I've been desperate to put it right by paying back the money. I was going to give it to George Benton, but he's dead. So I offered it to Jackie and she turned me down.'

Tania gasped. 'She actually refused to take a sum like that? I don't believe it.'

'It's true. I'm not lying.'

'No, I mean I don't believe her refusal was genuine. She wants you to think her honest so that you'll be lured in further—perhaps even marry her.'

'I don't believe that.'

'No, because you've formed a high opinion of her—exactly as you were meant to.'

'So you don't really like her after all?'

Tania hesitated before saying carefully, 'I'm not sure. She makes me cautious. But she's so clever and sharp-witted I wonder if she might be the right woman for you, because *she* could be the one who could make you stop your nonsense.'

This seemed to strike him. He considered thoughtfully before saying, 'My *nonsense*? I think you two must be in cahoots.'

'Why? Has she called you out on your nonsense too?'

'Not outright, but she implies it every time she opens her mouth.'

'Good for her.'

'Today she called me Prince Charmless.'

'Indeed? She actually said that?'

'Without any hesitation.'

Tania chuckled. 'Now I'm *really* beginning to like her.'

'I like her too,' Vittorio admitted. 'In some ways. But not in others. It comes and goes, and the feelings get intertwined.'

'You mean you have opposite feelings at the same time?'

'Yes—it's hard to know what to think of a woman with several different aspects.'

'That can be the best kind of woman,' Tania observed.

'Certainly the most interesting,' Vittorio murmured. 'And now I think I'll have an early night myself.'

'I hope you're not going to go knocking on her door.'

'I wouldn't dream of it. She and I are just friends. We've both made that very plain.'

'As long as you're both realists.'

'Not a doubt of it. Goodnight, Aunt.' He gave her a friendly peck on the cheek and departed.

Despite retiring early, Vittorio found that his need for sleep deserted him as soon as he went to bed. After tossing and turning for a while he rose, pulled on some jeans and a T-shirt, and went downstairs, then out into the garden.

He couldn't be certain what had disturbed him. Although he knew his aunt's words had touched a nerve, he was unwilling to admit how that touch had agitated him.

We're just friends. We've both made that very plain.

Was that being realistic? Despite her lack of conventional beauty, Jackie held an attraction for him that was unsettling—all the more so because he doubted if she felt the same way.

He walked for a long time before returning to his room and going back to bed. But still sleep evaded him, and he lay there restlessly for several hours until he nodded off just before it was time to get up.

Bad news was waiting for him when he went

down for breakfast. Leo, the permanent driver he employed, was feeling poorly.

'He can't drive you to Rome,' Tania told him. 'He isn't well enough.'

'No matter. I'll drive.' But he said it reluctantly. His disturbed night had left him feeling less than his best. But the trip was necessary, and he was sure he could be strong.

He reckoned it was the right decision as he observed Jackie on their journey. She had clearly done some research and knew where she wanted to visit.

'I'd like to see some more of the smaller shops,' she said after a few miles. 'The department stores are impressive, but a little shop can sometimes take you by surprise.'

'Yes, it can,' he said. 'I remember a little shop in London that took me *completely* by surprise. It was being run by a really prickly woman who trampled me underfoot, chucked me out and called me all kinds of names. And a few days later I was fool enough to bring her home with me. I can't think why...'

'I guess you just like being ill-treated,' she teased.

'That's right. And I'm sure she's got some more up her sleeve.'

'Never mind. If you fight back she'll probably make a run for it.'

'Don't you dare! Now I've got you here I'm going to keep you. You're my prisoner. Don't forget it.'

They laughed. And then they were in town, travelling the back streets where Vittorio discovered small businesses that impressed him in unfamiliar ways.

He watched as Jackie examined them, made notes, and drew his attention to things he hadn't noticed.

'You really *do* know your stuff,' he said at last as they got back into the car. 'I'm impressed.' He glanced around and said suddenly, 'Wait here, I'll be just a moment.'

On the far side of the road was a branch of the bank where he'd taken her the day before. He went in, stayed a few minutes, then returned to her.

'I've got something for you,' he said. 'Here.' He handed her a bundle of banknotes.

'But what—?'

'Now you're working for me, and that's your first commission.'

She flicked through the notes, astonished at the amount.

'It's more than I was expecting.'

'You're doing a good job. It's ten per cent of what I spent online under your advice.'

'We didn't actually agree my wages.'

'No, and if I was anything like the last man you worked for I'd cut the amount in half and defy you to challenge me. I wonder how far you'd get…'

'I never got anywhere arguing with Rik until you came and defended me,' she admitted.

'Right. But you're my employee now, and I don't expect you to work for nothing.'

'Well, if you put it like that—'

'You've *earned* that money, Jackie. Now, I'm starving,' Vittorio said. 'Just round that corner is a hotel with one of the best restaurants in Rome. Let's go. Unless you want to be difficult about that too?'

'No, I've had enough fun for today. Let's go.'

CHAPTER SEVEN

'YOU MEANT THAT about fun, didn't you? That's how you get your kicks—driving me mad.'

'Some people are more fun to drive mad than others.'

'You'd better watch out,' Vittorio said. 'It might be *my* turn to have fun.' He swung into a car park. 'Here we are.'

He escorted her inside the hotel and headed for the restaurant. When they were settled inside, Jackie's eyes widened at the sight of the menu.

'Best Roman cuisine,' Vittorio said. 'Does it tempt you?'

'Yes, it looks delicious.' He summoned the waiter and they ordered their food.

'Would you like wine?' he asked.

'Not really.'

'Me neither. I've got to drive us home. Let's have sparkling water.'

When the water arrived he filled both their glasses.

'To a successful business arrangement,' he said. They clinked glasses.

'Here's the food,' he said with relief as the waiter approached them.

The dishes that were laid before her looked delicious, and tasted that way too.

'Lovely!' she said.

'Good.'

He paused, and she had a strange feeling that he was summoning up his courage. When he spoke again he sounded uneasy.

'The fact is I wanted us to spend a little time together. Because I feel we need to talk.'

Jackie stared at him, puzzled. 'Do we?' she asked softly. 'You might say that we're the last people to want to talk.'

'But that's wrong. We connect because I'm the only person who knows exactly how you feel.'

'I don't think you *do* know how I feel. You can't imagine how all your money and luxury depresses me.'

'Because of your father and what was done to him? I understand how that makes you feel, but I wasn't the man who did it.' He took a deep breath. 'Why do you hate me, Jackie?'

She gave a brief ironic laugh. 'I guess it's because you're the one who's available to me. I can't chastise your father, because he isn't here. But you are, so I can—' She gave a slight shrug.

'Well, that's honest, anyway. So when you kick me in the teeth you just pretend you're kicking him?'

'I guess you're right.' She sighed. 'I keep telling myself to be reasonable, but then I remember Daddy's face looking the way I saw it so often. His life was terrible at the end. He'd lost everything.'

'He hadn't lost you. He had a daughter who cared for him.'

'Yes, but I couldn't fill all the empty spaces in his life. Even now I'm still trying to do my best by him.'

Vittorio closed his eyes. 'I can't describe hearing how my father had cheated his friend, stolen from him—what that did to me. I'd always admired him, practically worshipped him as a man to be trusted and honoured. Suddenly to discover that there was another truth about him—that he was capable of such a terrible action—'

Jackie was dismayed to see that he was shaking. She reached out and took his hand. 'It's not your fault,' she said.

He opened his eyes, gazing straight at her. 'I never thought to hear you say something like that,' he said.

'Well, it's true. You didn't steal the money.'

'But I lived on it. I grew up in luxury that I had no right to. And when I started out in business my father supported me financially. He couldn't have done that if he hadn't had that stolen money. The knowledge tortured me, but I had to keep my feelings to myself. I couldn't let him know while he was dying. And there's been nobody else I could talk to. Until now.'

'And talking helps, doesn't it?' she murmured. 'I never thought to say this, but in a strange way your loss has been greater than mine. My father remains in my heart just as he always was— loving, gentle, sweet-natured. That will never change. But you've lost the father you loved and admired. He's vanished and been replaced by an-other father who horrifies you. I do understand how that must be a miserable loss to you.'

From the way he stared at her she could tell she'd taken him completely by surprise.

'How did you…?' he murmured. 'However did you…?'

How did she know? she wondered. Perhaps it

was connected with the fierce sympathy for him that had risen in her so unexpectedly.

'You must have a gift for seeing into other people's hearts and minds,' he said.

She wasn't sure how to answer that. He was the last man in the world whose heart and mind she would have expected to see into.

'What is it?' he asked, looking at her face. 'Have I said something to disturb you?'

'No. I'm just thinking of the day we left England and Rik tried to stop me—the way you dealt with him. You said you'd do anything necessary to make him sorry he'd opened his big mouth, and that if he didn't get out you might do something you'd both regret. You were really scary.'

'And you thought that was the real me?'

'No—well, I did then. But now...'

He smiled. 'We all have different sides to our natures. I do have a side that's brutal, cruel, unforgiving, but I save it for creatures like him. Don't worry. You won't see it.'

'I'm not afraid,' she said, not entirely truthfully. 'As you say, we all have different sides. My own cruel, unforgiving side is lurking somewhere.'

'Hovering about *me* a lot recently, I guess?'

'I must admit I had it all geared up and ready for you. But now I know how different you are from what I expected...'

'You think perhaps I'm human and not an unfeeling robot?'

'I never thought you an unfeeling robot.'

'Liar.' But the word was said gently, and with a touch of humour.

'I guess I deserved that,' she said. 'If you were unfeeling you couldn't be suffering about your father as you do. You've really taken me by surprise.'

'I think we've taken each other by surprise.'

Vittorio rubbed a hand over his eyes, suddenly feeling wrung out by the emotions swirling in his head.

'Perhaps it's time we left,' he said.

His weariness was growing by the minute, and the tension of the evening was becoming more than he could cope with.

He signalled to the waiter, who approached with the bill.

Watching him, Jackie was struck by the heaviness in his manner, and the way he kept closing his eyes. Alarm began to grow in her.

At last the bill was paid.

'Time to go home,' he said.

'No.' She laid a hand on his arm. 'Vittorio, I don't think leaving is a good idea. You're in no fit state to drive.'

'But I haven't drunk any alcohol. You know that.'

'I know, but you're shattered. Your head's spinning.'

'You're right. I didn't sleep well last night.'

'You didn't sleep at *all*. You spent most of the night wandering in the grounds.'

'How the devil do you know that?'

'I saw you from my window—several times.'

'Yes, I suppose I was pretty obvious. I kept meaning to go inside and get some sleep, but somehow I couldn't make myself do it. I should have done. It's left me tired. But that's not the only thing. This evening—I've never talked about all this before.' He met her eyes. 'With you, it's different. You understand things that nobody else could, and I've said far more than I meant to say. It's hard to cope with what I... Things I said that I didn't mean to.'

She laid her hand over his. 'Can't I help you?'

'You've already helped by being you. At first

the past seemed to make us enemies, but it's also—' Words seemed to fail him.

'It's also opened a door of fellow feeling that we never imagined,' she said softly.

'Yes. Suddenly everything in the world seems to be different—I'm confused, but I'm also glad.'

'Perhaps it means that we really have managed to become friends?' she suggested tentatively.

He gave a wry smile. 'My best friend. Who would ever have imagined that?'

'Friendship can come out of the strangest places.'

'They don't come much stranger than ours.'

'And now, because I'm your friend, I'm telling you not to try to drive home tonight. It wouldn't be safe.'

'Don't panic. It'll be all right.'

'I don't think so.'

'You think I can't be trusted to drive properly?'

'I think you're not well enough. I've seen how you keep closing your eyes the way people do when their head's aching. You're in a bad way, and you could collapse at the wheel.'

'I promise not to. Now, let's go.'

Jackie took a deep breath. What she was about

to say was momentous. 'No. Vittorio, if you get into that car I'll call the police.'

He stared at her. 'Did I hear you right? That's the act of a *friend*, is it?'

'Yes. A friend who's trying to protect you from harm. I guess that's something you're not used to.'

'I'm certainly not used to people telling me what to do.'

'Don't worry. Now *I'm* here you'll get used to it.'

'So what's going to happen? Will *you* drive us home?

'No way. I'm not a confident driver, and I couldn't handle the Italian roads at night.'

'Then what are we going to do?'

'This is an hotel. We can stay the night and leave tomorrow. I'll go to Reception and book us two rooms.'

She tried to rise but his hand tightened on hers.

'I'll see to it,' he said.

He summoned the waiter and spoke in Italian. The waiter nodded and departed.

After a few moments he returned and addressed Vittorio, also in Italian.

'Oh, hell,' Vittorio groaned.

'What did he say?' Jackie asked. 'He spoke too fast for me to follow.'

'They don't have two rooms available. Just one. A double room.'

'Then take it,' she said. 'You need to go to bed. I can sleep in the car.'

'Why would you do that? Don't you trust me to behave decently?'

'Of course. It's just that— Well—'

'It's just that I'm on the point of collapse. I couldn't seduce you if I wanted to. You're quite safe.'

He rose to his feet.

Suddenly he staggered, reaching out to grasp at something. But there was nothing there. Jackie leapt to her feet, just managing to catch him in time to stop him falling.

She supported him to the reception desk, where he booked the double room. The receptionist cast curious glances back and forth between them, but said nothing.

'I wonder what he's thinking,' Jackie observed as they went up in the elevator.

'I imagine we can guess what he's thinking,' Vittorio growled. 'I planned to tell him you were my wife, but—'

'You're too well known around here to get away with that one,' she supplied. 'It wouldn't have worked. Much better for him to think I'm your latest lover.'

'That doesn't worry you?' he asked curiously.

'Why should it? Who cares about *my* reputation?' She gave a teasing chuckle. 'Yours is another matter. But I expect they're used to you appearing in this situation. All right—don't answer that.'

'You're enjoying this, aren't you?' he demanded.

'Well, I admit the sight of your face just now gave me a little cheeky pleasure.'

Cheeky, he thought wryly. If ever a word described someone that one described her. And she loved it.

Not for the first time he reminded himself to be on his guard. But his guard never really protected him against her.

At last the elevator reached their floor, stopping with a shudder that disturbed his balance again. Instinctively he seized hold of her. She clasped him in return, leading him out into the corridor.

'Room thirty-seven,' he gasped.

A notice on the wall gave her the direction of the room, which luckily wasn't far away. He reached into his pocket for the key and opened the door.

The room was large, dominated by a double bed. Slowly she led him across the floor so that he could slide onto it. He lay down with relief.

'Let me pull the duvet back so that you can lie underneath,' she said.

'No, I'm fine as I am. Thank you for getting me here.' He squeezed her hand. 'You're a life-saver. I'm sorry to do this to you.'

'No need to be sorry. Friends help each other.'

'I thought I'd be able to cope…'

'But what was there to cope with?'

Vittorio struggled to find the words to tell her about how his own thoughts and feelings had overcome him. But they were taking him over again.

'Forgive me…' was all he could say.

'There's nothing to forgive. We all have bad spells sometimes.'

'But I didn't handle it very well, did I?'

It was true, but she guessed he wasn't used to this kind of burden.

'Go to sleep,' she said. 'You need it.'

'I should call Tania first. She'll be expecting us home.'

'Yes, but tell her we can't come home because you've met a business associate and need to talk to him. We have to stay until your serious discussion is over. I'll be taking notes—like a secretary.'

'But where are we supposed to be sleeping?'

'You in here. Me in another room down the corridor.'

'But there isn't one.'

'Tania doesn't know that.'

He managed a smile. 'I guess you're right.'

She picked up the phone. 'Give me the number and I'll call her.'

Tania answered at once. Jackie immediately handed the phone to Vittorio, who managed to assume a vigorous, cheerful voice. Jackie couldn't follow every Italian word, but she could just about understand that he was doing as she'd advised.

'Thank you,' he said, hanging up at last. 'That's bought us a little time. You're a great organiser. Perhaps I really *should* go into business with you—not as an employee, but as a partner.'

'You never know. We might surprise each other.'

'I'm sure of it. Heavens, but my head is aching.' He closed his eyes and rubbed his hand over them.'

'Go to sleep,' she said. 'You'll feel better in the morning.'

'Where are you going to sleep?'

'There's a sofa over there.' She pointed to the sofa beneath the window.

Vittorio looked at it in concern. 'You'll never be comfortable there. It's too narrow and not long enough. Sleep here. This is a king-size bed. We can each take one side.'

'Not while you're lying diagonally on it,' she said. 'It doesn't leave me any room.'

He made some awkward movements to the side, but they seemed to tire him.

'It's no good,' she said. 'You need the whole bed. Stretch out and get comfortable.'

'But what about you? Who'll look after *you*?'

'I'm fine. You're the one who needs looking after. Shall I get something to cover you?'

'No, I'm warm enough. You go and lie down.'

He watched as she backed away and lay on the sofa. He felt as though he was sinking into a different world, overtaken by another self—one who was reaching out to her for safety. He frowned, trying to understand the mystery, but suddenly all thoughts vanished and a warm darkness descended on him.

Watching him, Jackie saw the exact moment when Vittorio fell into sleep. At last, she thought with relief. Now he could find a little peace.

But almost at once he began muttering in his sleep, then tossing and turning as though driven by some inner torment. It troubled her to see him floundering towards the very edge of the bed. At last one agitated movement brought him so near that he started to slide off, and she hurried across to hold him just in time.

'Steady,' she said.

'Mmm…' he murmured.

She couldn't tell if he'd heard her, or even knew she was there. His eyes were still closed but his hands grasped her, as if clinging to safety.

'Move back,' she urged him.

'Mmm?'

'Move back before you fall right off.'

He edged backwards, still holding her. She followed, joining him on the bed but not getting too close.

Suddenly he turned, throwing an arm over her.

His eyes were closed, and from his deep breathing she sensed that he was still asleep. She tried to nudge him away gently, but his arm tightened, drawing her close until his head rested on her shoulder.

Instinctively she wrapped her arms about him completely. She was amazed at the feeling that swept over her. This man, who always seemed so strong and determined, had aroused in her an instinct to protect. She knew that he needed the safety she could give him.

'Goodnight,' she whispered. 'Sleep well.'

His answer was a soft murmur. She couldn't make out the words, but she felt the movement of his lips against her neck and tightened her arms at the sensation that went through her. At once she felt his arms tighten in response.

He lay still for a while, but soon his lips began to move again. She leaned closer, trying to hear what he was saying, but the words were indistinguishable.

She could make out only one.

'Elena,' he murmured. 'Elena— Elena—'

Then he was silent again, leaving her wondering. Who was Elena? Was she the woman he'd spoken of? The one he'd found in bed with another man? Or was she some other ghost that haunted him?

He spoke again. 'Jackie— Jackie—'

'It's all right,' she said. 'I'm here.'

She wondered if he'd heard, and perhaps understood. Now he lay still. She listened intently for anything else he might say, but there was no more mention of Elena.

Who *was* she? And why was she with him in his head at this moment?

At last she felt her own body relax.

Her last thought before she drifted into sleep was that somehow this was perfect.

Vittorio had the sensation of being in another world. As time passed thoughts and impulses disturbed him more, driving sleep away, so that at last he opened his eyes.

He had no idea where he was. He only knew that he was being held in an embrace so comforting that blissful feelings streamed through him. But gradually everything became real and he discovered that he was lying in Jackie's arms.

At first he couldn't believe it. It was a dream.

It must be. But her warmth against him, the feel of her breasts beneath his head, were sensations of such sweetness that he was filled briefly with pleasure—and then with alarm.

How could he have let this happen? With what crazy lack of caution had he yielded to the desire to enfold her in his arms?

But at least she was asleep. If he was very cautious she might never know.

Moving with great care, he edged away, holding his breath lest she awake and discover how vulnerable he could be where she was concerned. That was something that must never happen. Inch by inch he drew back his arm and then his head, retreating to the safety of the far side of the bed.

There he lay tense and still, watching her for any sign of wakefulness. To his relief there was none. After a while he turned over and lay facing away from her, trying to get his thoughts and feelings in order. It wasn't easy…

Submerged in peaceful silence and sleep, Jackie was unaware of passing time until she felt herself returning to the world and opened her eyes. Memories were there of holding Vittorio in her arms, feeling him cling to her. But now she lay alone, and his back was turned to her.

A faint sense of disappointment was followed by a stronger feeling of relief.

He'd claimed her as his friend, but they didn't yet fully trust each other—and if he knew how she'd embraced him while he was unaware he might feel suspicious.

And he would not be pleased, she was sure. She remembered that he'd told her he wouldn't seduce her even if he wanted to.

He didn't want to. There was no doubt about that. If he'd woken to find himself in her arms he would have been embarrassed. Luckily fate had saved her from that disaster.

But then she remembered how she had enjoyed the sensation of holding him, the feel of his body against hers. And she knew there was another disaster that threatened her.

He stirred and turned to her. 'Ah, you're awake,' he said. 'Did you sleep well?'

'Perfectly, thank you.'

'No disturbing dreams?'

'Not a thing.'

'That's all right, then.'

She thought she detected relief in his voice. He couldn't have said more plainly that there was nothing between them but practical matters.

CHAPTER EIGHT

THE BEDSIDE PHONE RANG. Vittorio answered it and found himself talking to Tania, who sounded agitated.

'Are you *mad* to have that woman in your room?' Tania demanded.

'I told you we were both staying here.'

'But not in the same room. I just called the hotel to speak to her and they told me where she is. Have you *no* common sense?'

Vittorio ground his teeth and spoke quietly, hoping Jackie would hear little and understand less. 'There was only one room available. We had no choice.'

'Can you assure me you haven't lost control?'

'I'm not even tempted. She doesn't like me, and our relationship is strictly business.'

'So she hasn't even tried to put her arms around you?'

Vittorio ground his teeth. 'No,' he said. 'She hasn't. Goodbye, Aunt.'

He slammed down the phone.

'What's she so upset about?' Jackie demanded. 'I could hear her yelling even over the phone.'

'She's shocked because we're in the same room. She's concerned for your virtue.'

'Concerned for *yours*, you mean. Does she think I lured you into a double room because I have a scheme in mind?'

'We both know that you didn't want to share my room, disliking me as you do. I've reassured her that you don't want me.'

'But can she believe that *any* woman wouldn't seize the chance to seduce you and perhaps become a countess?'

'I guess not.'

Jackie began to chuckle. 'I can't believe this is happening. The idea of me acting the role of *femme fatale* is ludicrous.'

'Don't put yourself down,' he told her. 'You've got your attractions.'

'Not the kind likely to appeal to a man who can have any woman he wants,' she said cheerfully. 'I'm a realist. How much did you tell your aunt about what happened?'

'Nothing. She asked if you'd put your arms around me. I told her you hadn't.'

'Well, that's true. It was you who put your arms around *me*.'

He stared. 'Did I?'

'Don't worry. You didn't know what you were doing. I came over to the bed because you were close to the edge and I was afraid you'd fall. You were flailing wildly about and suddenly you grabbed hold of me. I couldn't get away.'

'Didn't you thump me hard enough?'

'Damn! I never thought of thumping you. Stupid of me.'

'Want to try now?'

'No, I'll save it and get some practice first. When I finally thump you—oh, boy, will you know you've been thumped!'

He grinned, but it soon faded.

'So we just lay there all night? Did I do anything? Say anything?'

She was tempted to ask him about Elena, but she backed away from the thought. Some deep instinct told her that she would be better not knowing.

'You muttered a load of nonsense,' she told him cheerfully.

'In other words typical me?'

'I didn't say that.'

'You didn't have to. What about you? Did you talk to me?'

'A little. You seemed so agitated that I told you it was all right.'

Suddenly he could hear exactly what she had said then. *It's all right. I'm here.* Again he felt the peaceful sensation that had overcome him earlier, as he'd lain in her arms. Everything had been all right because *she* was there.

So she knew that they had clung to each other by chance, but not how they had lain together so gently. It was a relief that she didn't recall the moment and blame him for it, but also disappointing that she didn't share the memory of it with him.

He rose and went to the door. 'I'll go and sort the bill downstairs,' he said. 'Then we can leave.'

'Let's have some breakfast first,' she said. 'We don't want you falling asleep at the wheel.'

Turning to leave, he gave her a wry grin. 'I'll forget you said that.'

He closed the door softly behind him.

Somehow she must banish from her mind the sweet memory of lying in his arms. A shared memory would have been lovely, but he seemed not to know everything that had happened between them. So it would be dangerous for her to brood on it lest her feelings riot out of control.

After that it seemed best to be businesslike. Downstairs they ate breakfast, discussed sensible matters and left the hotel.

Vittorio's headache had gone and he was relieved to find himself driving at the height of his ability. That was what a restful night did. It was a reason to thank Jackie, but he mustn't tell her, he warned himself wryly . She would be sure to turn it against him in a cheeky challenge. There was just no way of coping with this infuriating woman.

But she was more than infuriating. Alarming, troublesome, teasing, tempting, alluring. And never more than one of them for five minutes at a time.

They were almost home before Vittorio broke the comfortable silence between them. 'I hope we haven't got another problem waiting for us.'

'What kind of problem?'

'Tania. How do we cope with her suspicions about last night?'

'That's easy,' Jackie said. 'We assume indifference.'

'You mean we don't speak to each other? As if we've quarrelled?'

'No, that would only convince her she's right. When we get there, just follow my lead.'

As he'd been doing for the last few days, he reflected ruefully.

At last the car drew up outside the castle—and there was Tania, standing by the door.

As they headed towards her Jackie said, loudly enough to be heard, 'You're quite wrong about this, Vittorio. It would be a very poor purchase and not worth the money.'

Catching on quickly, Vittorio enthusiastically joined the conversation. 'Of course I respect your opinion, Jackie, but I think that item would be a good buy.'

They continued this back and forth until they were at the front door, where Tania was still waiting to greet them.

'What are you two arguing about now?'

'Ask her—*she's* the expert,' Vittorio said. 'I don't even understand.'

'Do you *ever* understand?' Jackie demanded. 'That thing looked good, but you're too easily fooled.'

'What thing?' Tania asked.

'Let *her* tell you,' Vittorio said. 'I'm going to get a drink.'

He vanished, leaving the two women regarding each other.

'What thing are you arguing about?' Tania asked.

'I can't even remember. We've seen so many things that he might buy, but he's being awkward.'

'Has he been misbehaving?' Tania asked.

'Only in one sense. He thinks he knows everything about business, but he doesn't understand as much as he thinks he does. And if you dare tell him he's got it wrong he gets insulted.'

'Then perhaps you shouldn't tell him.'

'Oh, I think I should,' Jackie declared. 'It's not good to let a person think they're always right about everything. Of course, certain people are *always* going to be convinced of that, no matter what.'

'It's lucky he can't hear you saying that,' Tania observed.

'He's heard me say worse. He knows I'm not afraid to condemn him. Luckily he doesn't care about my opinion any more than I care about his.'

'I was rather worried about you two being in the same bedroom last night.'

'Don't be. Nothing happened.'

Tania still looked unconvinced.

'Look, Vittorio doesn't want anything from me except efficiency in business. And I don't want anything from him either. So don't worry. I'm not trying to drag him up the aisle.'

Tania gave her an amused look. 'Am I supposed to believe that?'

'Believe it. All the others may yearn to be a countess, but I don't. He's quite safe from me.'

'Has he told you about how lively things are going to get soon?'

'No. Why? What's going to happen?'

'Every June we give a ball. Everyone comes from miles around. It's a huge, exciting event. You'll have great fun choosing something to wear.'

'Do people wear fancy dress?

'Some of them. Some wear conventional ball gowns and some wear historical costumes. We even have a Lady Nanetta costume you could wear.'

'I'll really look forward to this ball.'

'And I want you to enjoy it. Ah, there's Gina. Please excuse me, Jackie, but I must get on.'

After Tania had left Jackie headed up to her room, intending to type up the notes she'd made in Rome. But after a few minutes there came a soft knock on the door. She found Vittorio standing there, and stood back to let him in.

'That was a brilliant idea of yours,' he said. 'If we're arguing about business there can't be anything else between us.'

'I promised her I wasn't trying to drag you up the aisle.'

'I know. I heard you.'

'You—? You were *listening*?'

'Of course. Just behind the door. You're more fun to eavesdrop on than anyone I know. Nobody else complains about me with as much imagination as you do. But I seem to have improved in your estimation. Saying I always think I'm right isn't as bad as saying I'm cold and arrogant.'

'All right—enjoy your laugh. I have to be tough on you in front of Aunt Tania so that she knows I'm not one of the crowd chasing you. That way you can use me as a defence.'

He nodded. 'And you're the perfect defence.' He

hesitated before saying, 'Are you all right after what happened last night?'

'*Nothing* happened last night,' she said firmly.

'No—of course nothing did. I only meant—Well, it was nice to be in your arms.'

So he *did* know, she thought.

'Yes,' she agreed. 'It was nice and friendly.'

He regarded her for a moment before saying softly, 'Just friendly?'

'I don't know,' she murmured. 'It's hard to say.'

He didn't answer at first. Then he placed his fingers under her chin and raised it, before dropping his head to brush her lips with his own.

'I'm sorry,' he whispered. 'I shouldn't have done that. I just wanted to know—'

'Yes,' she said. 'But it's not possible. We *can't* know.'

'Can't we?'

'It's too soon.'

'Too soon can be the best time—when you're learning about each other and want to know more. Am I offending you? Do you want to push me away?'

'No—no—'

He lowered his head again, placing his mouth on hers more intensely than before, although not

enough to alarm her. She responded with pleasure, moving her lips gently against his and relishing his instant reaction. She felt his arms
tighten and a tremor go through his body.

Where was this leading? Control was slipping
away from both of them.

And then— 'I'm sorry,' Vittorio said, releas-
ing her. 'That was thoughtless and selfish of me.'

He stepped back, leaving a clear gap between
them.

'Was it?' she asked, bewildered.

'You're vulnerable. I should have remembered—'

'But—'

'Forgive me, Jackie. I didn't mean to— Just
forget it ever happened.'

'Forget what? How can I forget something that
didn't happen?' she said in a freezing voice.

He backed further away. 'You're right—it
didn't. It couldn't happen because we have to
understand— I'd better go.'

He turned and abruptly left the room.

Jackie stood motionless, possessed by such a
fury that she was tempted to hurl something at
the door. She restrained the impulse, lest he hear
and realise how he had affected her.

She could hardly believe how intensely she had responded to him. The touch of his lips, the feel of his embrace had started an excitement that had spread swiftly through her, igniting a fierce response.

The best part of it had been her awareness of a response in *him*. In one blazing, beautiful moment she'd known that he wanted her as much as he'd managed to make her want him. But then, in an assertion of strength, he'd silenced his own desire, rejecting her with a pretence of chivalry that didn't fool her for a moment.

Did he *know* that he'd inflamed her passion before rejecting her? Or didn't he care about her feelings while he was protecting his own?

No, she thought bitterly. He didn't care. He didn't care about her at all. To yield to his own needs would have meant letting her know that she had a kind of power over him. And that was something that he wouldn't risk.

All the power had to be on *his* side. He'd left to protect himself, not her.

Well, two could play the power game!

The next morning Jackie went downstairs to find only Tania waiting for her in the breakfast room.

'Your argument must have been fiercer than it seemed,' she said. 'Vittorio's gone away on estate business.'

'Doesn't he often have to do that?'

'Sometimes. There's a tiny village on the far side of his land, and he needs to stay there for a couple of days.'

Before Jackie could reply her cell phone rang. Answering it, she found herself talking to Gary, a salesman who had frequently called in to the shop in London, usually with good products to offer. They were on friendly terms.

'Hello, Gary,' she said cheerfully.

'It was quite a shock to find you missing. Are you going to be over there long?'

'Hard to say.'

'Well if you return to England, don't forget me.'

'Not a chance. It'll be nice to see you again.'

She hung up.

Tania was arranging things on the breakfast table.

'That looks lovely,' Jackie said, regarding the food. 'When I've had breakfast it's time I started attending to some business.'

'What business?'

'Vittorio has left me in charge of a new department in his store. There's a lot to do, and I must go into Rome and get to work.'

'You don't have to if you don't want to,' Tania said.

'But I *do* want to. He's paying me well and I'm going to work hard and earn it. I'm really looking forward to it.'

It was true. Taking charge of the new department could be exactly the kind of pleasure she would most enjoy. But instinct warned her of another aspect.

After what had happened in the hotel Vittorio had gone away in order to avoid her. Well, if he thought she was going to play the rejected woman—watching for his return, wondering when he would find time for her—he was mistaken.

Tania called her a taxi and she was soon on her way to Rome. Entering the store, she wondered what reaction would greet her. Had Vittorio really declared her authority as definitely as she'd believed he had?

Her fears were eased at once. The staff in her department greeted her respectfully—especially Lisa, the chief assistant.

'We have some new stock just delivered,' she said eagerly. 'We were about to start unpacking it.'

'Splendid. Let's get going.'

The next few hours were delightful. The new arrivals were glass items, elegant and expensive, not just dishes but also small statues of animals.

'These are incredible,' Jackie said, lifting one up to study it. 'I think this is a lion...'

'Yes, and this one is a tiger,' Lisa said. 'Over here we have a horse and a bear.'

'All made of glass and *so* lovely. Where shall we put them?'

'I think we already have buyers,' Lisa said suddenly.

Jackie looked up to find a husband and wife descending on them. They were entranced by the statues and insisted on buying every one.

'I can't believe that really happened,' Jackie said in a daze. 'One minute we'd unpacked them—the next moment they were gone.'

'You must have bought the right thing,' Lisa said brightly. 'We'd better replace them quickly.'

In a moment Jackie was back on the computer, contacting the manufacturer and concluding another purchase.

'I've ordered three times as many,' she said. 'And they'll be delivered tomorrow.'

Her staff cheered. Jackie wondered if she had ever known a happier occasion in her life. To be in charge, to see everything work out so well, to know that she was more than capable of handling the situation—all this inspired a pleasure and a satisfaction that was almost beyond her understanding.

She plunged back into work, loving every moment. When the time came to leave she was almost reluctant.

'I know the store's closing, but I've got so much I want to do,' she said, indicating the computer.

'You could stay the night,' Lisa told her. 'Signor Vittorio has a place where he sleeps.'

'Then I'll use that.'

Jackie called Tania, wondering if Vittorio had arrived home yet. But she told her he wasn't expected for another day.

'I'm staying here at the store tonight,' she said.

'But are you sure?' Tania asked. 'I can arrange a taxi—'

'I must stay. There's so much work to do that I can't leave. Vittorio gave me this job so that I can make money for him, and I mustn't neglect it.'

'Very well. I'll explain to him when he returns.'

A tiny bedroom, almost as small as a cupboard, was attached to Vittorio's office. Clearly this was an emergency refuge, for use only when he was so submerged in work that nothing else mattered.

The bed was narrow, but comfortable. Jackie had worked late before retiring for the night. Now it felt good to brood over the success of the day. She looked forward to displaying everything to Vittorio.

She was up early next morning, greeting the staff, watching closely as their work got under way.

'The delivery is here,' Lisa said excitedly.

'Great. We'll get it displayed at once.'

'But there is so much!' Lisa protested. 'Where can we put it all?'

'Over there,' Jackie said, pointing to a large cabinet. 'Move the stuff out of that and we'll have room for everything.'

They got to work. Jackie watched, delighted at the way everything was changing for the better—not just in the store but in her life.

'It's going to look wonderful,' Lisa declared. 'We'll have to move some more things but—'

Lisa checked herself, clearly distracted by something she'd seen a few feet away.

Turning, Jackie saw Vittorio. After a glance at his grim face Lisa scuttled away.

'Tania told me I'd find you here,' he said. 'She says you stayed all night.'

He was scowling, and he sounded angry.

Jackie regarded him, puzzled. 'That's right,' she said. 'I got so involved in my work here that I wanted to concentrate on it, so I was here all night. I'm sure you're glad to know I've been working hard.'

'I'm not sure I'm *glad* about what I'm seeing. You've taken over and changed a great deal here. I don't remember us discussing it.'

'We didn't discuss it. There was a lucky chance—new stock that sold well. I've simply bought some more.'

'Which I can see is being delivered now. When did you order it?'

'Yesterday.'

'Surely not. It can hardly have been delivered so soon.'

'Let me show you.'

She accessed the computer, bringing up details

of the order, which Vittorio regarded with growing shock.

'Look at the price of that stuff!' he breathed. 'You've bought so *much* of it, and paid all that extra money for a fast delivery. And you've done it without consulting me. Are you trying to make me bankrupt?'

'Are you saying you can't afford it? This from the man who tried to bribe me with a million pounds?'

'Don't dare say that. I didn't try to *bribe* you. I just want to pay you what you're entitled to. This is quite different. It isn't about money. It's about you trying to push me aside and take over.'

'I'm not *taking over*. I'm just exercising the authority you gave me.'

'I never meant it to be like *this*.'

Her temper rose. Everything had seemed so wonderful before, and now he was ruining it.

She faced him with blazing eyes. 'You said I'd be in charge of my own department. That I'd have a team who would take my orders. I thought you meant it—but perhaps I should have understood you better.'

'What the devil do you mean by *that*?'

'I should have realised that you're a man who

says what suits him but doesn't mean a word of it. When I ask you to live up to your promises, you object. When I stand up to you, you can't cope.'

His face tightened. 'We've made jokes about you being a bully,' he snapped, 'but it's *not* a joke. That's what you are.'

'I do *not* bully my staff.'

'No, but you're trying to bully *me*.'

'Then we're equal. We're both bullies. That's why we can never get things right between us.'

'Don't tempt me to fire you!' he snapped.

'You don't need to. I resign here and now. It's over. Finished.'

'No, wait— Jackie—'

'I mean it. I *won't* put up with you dictating to me. It's not what we agreed.'

'We didn't agree about you meeting men behind my back, but that didn't stop you.'

'What?'

'That's why you're here, isn't it? This guy named Gary called and you hurried here to meet him yesterday. And you stayed the night,'

'Did Tania—?'

'Yes, she heard you talking to him. Where is he?'

'In England.'

He paused to give her a bitter glance, before turning away and heading for his office, where he wrenched open the door to the tiny bedroom. He saw that it was empty.

'Where is he?'

'He's in England,' Jackie said furiously. 'He never came here and I haven't seen him. I came here to get on with some *work*. Vittorio, you're out of your mind. It was pure chance that he rang when he did.'

'And you said you looked forward to seeing him.'

'Only when I go back to England—which will now be soon. I'm finished here. I can't work for you any more. You're impossible.'

He took hold of her at once. 'I don't want you to go.'

'I didn't ask what you want. I'm going.'

'You're not.' His grip tightened. 'We made an agreement—'

'Which *you* have broken.'

'That's not true. I promised you status and authority—'

'And you didn't mean a word of it.'

'You think so? Let's see if I can change your

mind.' He glanced out through the door, where Lisa could just be seen. *'Lisa!'*

Lisa entered the office, looking back and forth between them with a puzzled frown.

'I want to talk to the other staff,' Vittorio said. 'See how many of them you can get in here.'

'Some of them are busy serving.'

'Just get the ones who are free. I have an important announcement to make.'

When Lisa had gone Jackie asked, 'What are you going to tell them?'

'Wait and see.'

'But isn't it something I need to know?'

'You mean I need your *agreement*? No way. Listen to what I have to say, and then you'll know everything.'

'But you can't—'

'Don't tell me what I can and can't do. I'm your boss. Whatever I say, you'll have to accept it.'

She could have screamed with frustration. His meaning was all too clear.

Rather than let her embarrass him by resigning, he was going to shame her by dismissing her in front of an audience. She'd thought him better, more generous than this.

The rest of the staff were coming into the room.

Vittorio's grip on her arm remained firm as he greeted them.

'Gather round, everyone. I've got an announcement to make which will probably surprise you, but it's the inevitable result of Jackie's actions over the last two days.'

Jackie tensed in anguish. Could this *really* be happening?

'You've all seen how she's plunged herself into work,' Vittorio continued. 'Increasing the stock, changing the arrangements. I reckon there's only one response I can make to everything she's done…' He took a deep breath. 'So I've decided to promote her. From now on she'll have a place on the leadership team and a significant payrise.'

A friendly cheer broke out, backed up by the sound of applause.

Jackie barely heard. She was staring at Vittorio, trying to believe the words that were spinning in her head.

He met her eyes, his own gleaming with ironic humour and something else that she wasn't sure she could understand. He leaned down, murmuring, 'Now you know what I wanted to say. Do you have any objections?'

'I don't know.'

Everyone crowded round her, patting her, con-gratulating her.

'I don't *think* I have any objections,' she said.

He leaned down again and whispered in her ear. 'Think about it and tell me later.'

'Yes,' she agreed.

Like everything else between them, it would have to be decided on later.

CHAPTER NINE

'WE'LL SETTLE THE details later,' Vittorio told his employees. 'For the moment all you need to know is that Jackie is a great power.'

He took Jackie's hand so that she had no choice but to follow him out of the building to a small restaurant nearby. 'Now for something to eat,' he said. 'After that I need something to boost my strength,' he added when they were settled at the table.

'So do I. You really enjoyed catching me on the wrong foot, didn't you?'

He turned, regarding her with an indignation that amazed her.

'*What* did you say?' he demanded. 'You think I caught you on the wrong foot? No way. You threatened to leave and I responded by improving your position. Who won? I'd say *you* did.'

'Oh, come on—'

'*You* come on. You've transformed the department to suit your own ideas. When I ventured to protest you reduced me to silence. Let's be clear who's the strong one—and it's not me.'

His tone was almost light, yet she detected a hint of definite annoyance.

She smiled at him. 'For a moment I thought you were really angry,' she said.

'No, I know how to accept defeat.'

'I wasn't trying to defeat you—'

'We'll have to disagree about that. But the sight of your face when I said you were promoted is something I'll always remember.'

'Did you really mean it?' she asked. 'It sounds so incredible.'

'Then you'll have to prove I got it right, won't you?'

'I'll try. And, however it may seem, I really *am* grateful. I thought you were going to dismiss me—'

'No way. You're far too valuable for me to risk throwing you away. You're going to make me a big profit.'

'But think of the money you've risked by doubling my salary.'

'True. I shall have to work you twice as hard.' He grinned. 'Perhaps you should be afraid.'

'The one thing I *can't* imagine is being afraid of you.'

'Is that true?' he asked ironically.

It wasn't, but just now it seemed better to be tactful.

'True enough,' she said. 'Thank you for what you did today. I'm really grateful.'

'So we're friends again?' he asked.

'I guess we are.'

He smiled and began to lean towards her. For a moment she thought he meant to kiss her, but suddenly his face lit up.

'Stefano!' he cried. 'Fancy finding you here!'

Looking around, Jackie saw a good-looking man in his thirties standing a few feet away. The man approached the table and sat down in the chair that Vittorio had pulled out for him.

When they had clapped each other on the shoulder Vittorio said, 'Jackie, let me introduce you to my great friend—Barone Stefano Fedele.'

She shook his hand. 'Signor Barone.'

'Call me Stefano,' he said, kissing her hand theatrically. 'A friend of Vittorio's is a friend of mine.'

'Come and eat with us,' Vittorio said.

'I would love to, but I'm in a hurry. I'll see you at the ball.' He grinned cheekily. '*If* I'm invited.'

'You know you are. Always!'

'It'll be a great evening. As always. Now, I must go, but I look forward to seeing you.'

He hurried away.

'What a nice man,' Jackie said.

'Yes, he's got a lot of charm. Too much sometimes.'

'Too much?'

'A bit of a flirt. Did you notice how he kissed your hand?'

'Yes. Charming…'

'His name means "faithful". And never did a man have a less appropriate name. He's what is politely known as a playboy. The impolite version you can probably imagine.'

'Okay, you've warned me. I won't go falling for him.'

'Do you *ever* fall for any man?' he asked with a touch of humour.

'That depends on the man. Sometimes I have to be wary of a man because he's nice enough to tempt me. Others don't fit the bill.'

'How long does it take you to decide which category a guy fits into?'

'It varies. Sometimes ten seconds is enough, and sometimes I have to give him a chance.'

She sounded well experienced in dealing with unwanted men, Vittorio thought. He wondered in which of the two categories she would place himself, and was briefly tempted to ask her—in a jokey manner. But caution made him resist the temptation.

He was still troubled by the memory of the kiss he had ventured to give her two days ago, and how it had affected him so intensely that he'd backed off in fear—rejecting her and rejecting his own inner self that had started to make him aware of things that troubled him.

He longed to know if the memory haunted her too. But he had an uneasy feeling that perhaps it amused her.

They barely spoke on the journey home. Once there, he returned to work in his office and she joined Tania, who was deep in planning for the ball.

'Things are building up,' she said. 'We've started receiving replies to the invitations. All acceptances. Nobody ever refuses.'

She showed Jackie the guest list, on which

some names had been marked with a tick to indicate acceptance.

'You can tick Baron Stefano Fedele,' Jackie said. 'We met him this afternoon and he's looking forward to it.'

'You met him? Tell me more.'

Beaming, Tania listened as Jackie described the meeting.

'He's a good friend,' Tania said. 'And we need some of those to counterbalance the crowd of women who'll turn up and flaunt themselves. I wish we could keep them out, but they come from notable families and we have to invite them all out of good manners. We can't tell them to leave their daughters behind!' Tania sighed. 'By far the worst woman we will be forced to endure is the woman who betrayed my nephew in the past.'

'She's actually *invited*?' Jackie gasped. 'After what she did?'

'Her husband is the Duke of Revendo. His family have always been part of high society, invited to all notable occasions. If they were left out everyone would know why. And the gossip would be terrible. Vittorio simply can't risk having people giggle about how he was rejected by the Duchess because he wasn't noble enough.'

Jackie was stunned. In her mind Vittorio was the stern, determined man who had rescued her from Rik and used his strength to defend her. They had shared occasional jokes, and the night he had collapsed in the Rome hotel had shown her a gentler side to him. But never for a moment had he seemed as vulnerable as Tania's words now suggested.

Had something changed for him that night? Had there been a moment when he'd dreamed the woman lying beside him was the beloved he'd lost? Had she, Jackie, looked different to him ever since?

She couldn't tell. But suddenly, with all her heart, she longed to know.

Tania hesitated before asking quietly, 'Is everything all right between you and Vittorio—about that other man?'

'There isn't another man. I know you heard me talk to Gary on the phone, but I didn't go into town to meet him. He's in England.'

'Oh, dear. I'm afraid I told Vittorio about his call and...' She sighed helplessly.

'And he thought the worst because he thinks no woman can be trusted. Why is he so sure of that? I know about this woman who deceived him with another man, but surely he's had time to grow out of that?'

'You're right. It's not just her. It was his mother too. He adored her. They were very close, and he felt he was the centre of her life until she deserted him.'

'She ran away with another man?'

'No, she died in childbirth—but the baby came from an affair with another man. The baby died too. They're buried together. I once saw Vittorio looking at that grave, and what I read in his face was heartbreaking. He loved her so much, and had always felt she loved him, and yet she lay there with another son in hers arms for ever.'

'But that's terrible,' Jackie said. 'How could he bear it?'

'It still causes him great pain. To be fair, I can't entirely blame his mother. His father was never faithful. He slept with dozens of other women and she took refuge in affairs of her own. They did it to get back at each other, but it was their child who suffered.'

'And it's still with him, even now?'

'Yes. If even his *mother* couldn't be trusted, then he believes no woman can be trusted.'

'And then there was this girl who betrayed him?'

'Worst of all is our being forced to receive her at the ball. But now I suggest an early night,' Tania said. 'From now on we will have a mountain of work to do.'

As they left the room Jackie and Tania continued to discuss the ball for a while longer before Vittorio joined them. Tania was talking enthusiastically about the costume she planned to wear before turning to Jackie.

'Jackie, I really think you should wear Lady Nanetta's gown. What about you Vittorio? Modern evening dress?'

'No, if Jackie agrees I will be taking my costume from the guy in the picture next to Lady Nanetta. Let's have a look at him now.'

Vittorio and Jackie went to the gallery to find the picture he was talking about. Jackie studied it with fascination. He was a tall man in Regency attire. The trousers were white, the jacket dark blue.

'You're going to wear *that*?' Jackie asked.

'If I can get into it. I think I probably can.'

'All the women who want to be in your harem will love it.'

'If I wanted a harem I'd be flattered by that remark. As it is, I'll remind you that you're here to protect me.'

Tania appeared in the doorway of the gallery then, beckoning Vittorio over. He went to talk to her and Jackie went up to her room. She wanted to be alone to get her thoughts together.

She had been troubled before by a guilty feeling that she was enjoying this luxury at the expense of her father's suffering.

She reached into her bag. After few moments she found what she was seeking and took it out to study it. It was a photograph that she had taken of her father ten years ago. There was George's face, gazing back at her, his eyes as gentle and warm as she remembered them.

'That's a nice picture,' said a deep voice.

Turning, she saw Vittorio standing close. He had slipped in through the half-open door and come over to her without her realising.

'It's my father,' she said.

'I know. I recognise him from the picture my father had of him.'

'You have a picture of my father? Oh, please, let me see it.'

'I'll get it.'

He left her room, heading across the corridor to his own.

Impulsively she followed him, and saw him going through a drawer, turning out papers. He handed a photograph to her, and she stared at it in astonishment.

'Yes, that's Daddy. And the other man is your father.'

'You say that as though you've seen him before.'

'The day after we met I went online to look up the Counts of Martelli. I was curious about you.'

'And you wanted to know if I was who I'd said I was, or whether I'd been telling you a pack of lies?'

He spoke cheerfully, without resentment, but she felt self-conscious enough to say, 'I didn't know you so well in those days.'

'And now you know me better you trust me even less?' he said, in the same light-hearted voice.

'It depends on the circumstances. Sometimes I think you're the biggest fraudster ever. At other

times our minds seem to connect so well that…'
She paused.

'That you don't believe me to be so bad after
all?'

'You probably knew that already.'

'Well, whatever you think of me it's pretty obvious that our fathers got on well. This picture
says a lot, don't you agree? It was taken in Italy.
You can see that they were good friends.'

The two men faced the camera, grinning, arms
raised exuberantly, clearly rejoicing in each other's company.

'They *do* look happy together,' she murmured.

'Yes, they do. There's no hint there of what was
to happen later.'

'No. I don't think I ever saw Daddy enjoy himself so much.'

'Nor me. My father was a serious man, and an
honourable one—or so I once thought. I don't recall ever seeing him bouncing with glee like this.'

In silence they met each other's eyes. Each
knew what the other was thinking, but neither
spoke. No words were necessary.

At last she said, 'Do you have any more pic-
tures of your father?'

He rummaged in the drawer and produced

a head shot. It depicted what Vittorio had described—a serious, honourable man, who looked
incapable of any shameful action.

Jackie gazed at him, hoping her desperate emotion couldn't be seen on her face.

You did it, she thought. *You ruined my lovely
father's life and got away with it. And your son
thinks he can put it right with money because
he can't understand that nothing can ever put it
right.*

She handed the picture back.

Vittorio put it aside and clasped his hand over
hers. 'I'm sorry,' he said.

'Don't be. He did it. Not you.'

'If only there was something you would let me
do—'

'Stop it. *Stop it!*' she said quickly. 'Don't talk
about it again.'

'Yes, it's dangerous ground, isn't it? Jackie, will
we ever be able to risk treading that ground?'

'I don't know. Sometimes I think not—but how
can we know?'

'We can't know,' he said. 'We can only hope.'

'Yes,' she murmured. 'But for the moment hope
will take time.'

She hurried away, escaping to her own room

and locking the door. She seized her father's picture again and looked at it for a long moment.

'Oh, Daddy,' she whispered, 'what shall I do? Please tell me?'

But if his loving eyes were sending her a message she could not understand it.

The next morning Tania departed to visit friends overnight. Jackie and Vittorio returned to Rome. She had noticed a small empty shop on a corner, and become fascinated by the idea of taking it over.

'It might be useful as a showcase for people who don't want to go to a huge store,' she said.

'That's an interesting idea,' Vittorio replied.

They spent some hours in the shop, which belonged to the man who lived above it. Vittorio made an offer that he accepted and the deal was quickly settled.

He finished the day by taking her into a nearby jeweller's shop and buying her a diamond necklace.

'That's—that's very generous of you,' she stammered.

'You've more than earned it. And if anyone asks you, tell them it was a gift from me.'

Thus supporting their pretence of being a couple, she thought. It was a severely calculated act, and there was nothing emotional about the gift, but she had to admit that it was beautiful and looked lovely about her neck.

'I need to call in to the bank,' he said. 'I won't be long.'

He was back in a moment, with an unusual, slightly mischievous look on his face that puzzled her.

'What's happened?' she asked.

'It'll tell you when we get home.'

'Why do you have to make a mystery of everything?'

'Because when a man knows he's doing the right thing he has to make sure nothing can get in the way.'

'Am I *likely* to get in the way of the right thing?'

'Let's say we don't always see eye to eye about what the right thing is.'

She longed to press him further, but felt it would be wise to wait until their journey was over.

At last they arrived home and he followed her to her room.

'Tell me,' she said, smiling with anticipation.

He produced a piece of paper from his pocket and handed it to her.

'You'll find the answer there,' he said.

Eyes wide, she opened it. In a moment she was overtaken by shock.

'What—what is this?'

'It's your bank statement.'

'But—how come—?'

The statement clearly indicated receipt of over a million British pounds converted to euros.

'How does that money come to be there?' she demanded.

'I put it there. You're entitled to it.'

'But I told you I wouldn't take it. You have no right to force it on me.'

'And you have no right to refuse it. It was something I *had* to do, Jackie.'

'Why? So that you can feel better about your thief of a father? I told you *no!* If you could have given it to Daddy that would have been right, but he's dead and it's too late. You can't ease his suffering now and you can't buy me off.' She looked at the statement again. 'When did you do this?'

'Yesterday. I called the bank and instructed them on the phone.'

'You dared to—?'

'I told them to take that money out of my account and transfer it to yours.'

'But I've told you a dozen times not to do anything like that,' she snapped.

'Don't *my* wishes count for anything?'

'Not when they make so little sense.

'No, it doesn't make any sense to you that I loved my father and can't forgive what was done to him. If he was alive and could accept the money himself, that would be fine. But he can't. And now it's your own feelings that matter to you. And your father's.'

'Jackie—'

'Listen to me, Vittorio, and try to understand. The only thing that would ever make things right would be if you gave back the money not to me but directly to Daddy.'

'But that's impossible!'

'Yes. It's impossible. And that's why we'll never agree about this. When you put that money in my account you did something bad and arrogant.'

She came to stand before him, regarding him with a cynical face.

'What trick did you play to get a copy of my bank statement? Do people obey you in everything?'

He seemed uneasy. 'Not everything, but they do know me at the bank. I told them that you're my fiancée.'

'You told them what?'

'I said we were going to be married.'

'And what happens when they find out you were lying?'

'I wasn't lying. Marriage would be the best thing for us, and I count on your good sense to make you see it.'

'Are you out of your *mind*? We're the last people in the world who should think of marriage.'

'On the contrary. We're the first. From the moment we met we've understood each other—'

'*No*. It's seemed like that sometimes, but all you understand is wanting your own way. This isn't about *my* father's suffering—it's about *your* father. You want to restore your image of him as a decent and honourable man. And I can't let you do that because of how guilty it would make me feel to let you buy me off. You don't understand how I could actually turn down your money. Tell me, Vittorio, has anyone in your whole life actually refused to let you buy them?'

'No,' he said, white-faced. 'People are sensible about money.'

'But I'm not sensible and hard-hearted. I'm human. I've got feelings. What would you know about that?'

'And what would *you* know about feelings?' he raged. 'The only one you have is hatred.'

'Just for you.'

'All this because I asked you to marry me?'

'But you *didn't* ask me. You told me that the decision had been taken—after you'd informed the rest of the world. Well, now you'll have to tell them that you got it wrong, because I'd sooner die than marry you. I want nothing from you— not your money *or* this.'

She seized the box containing the diamond necklace.

'Take it,' she said.

But he backed away, holding up his hands to ward her off. 'Jackie, please don't do this.'

'I said take it.'

She wrenched open the box, tore out the necklace and hurled it at him. He managed to seize it in time to stop it hitting his face, and tossed it back into the box.

'We won't talk about this now,' he said. 'Not while you're in such a state. When you've calmed down you'll see matters more rationally.'

'Don't fool yourself. I know what you mean by "rationally". It means me seeing things from your point of view. Well, that will never happen. I can't stand the sight of you, I can't bear to be in the same room as you, and I never want to be with you again, you monstrous bully. Now, get out. I'm leaving.'

He left at once, anxious to get away from the hate-filled atmosphere.

Jackie watched him go and locked the door. At all costs he must not be allowed to return.

Oh, how she hated him. Once she might have loved him, but not any longer. Not now that he'd insulted her with an offer of marriage and money. It might seem crazily illogical, but this man had inflamed her feelings and then tried to take possession of her as a business venture.

Now there was only one thing left that she could do.

She had to get out of here. To get away from him and fast.

She threw her things into her suitcase and checked to be sure she had her passport and purse.

It would be a long walk to Rome, and briefly she considered asking Leo, the chauffeur, to drive her. But she abandoned the idea as risky. She must walk.

Before leaving, she wrote a note to Vittorio.

I'm sure you realise why I have to go. It wasn't working between us and it never would.

She slipped it under his bedroom door. Then she went to the back staircase, where she could descend unseen. At the bottom she found herself near the back door. She would be able to slip out unnoticed.

She began to walk. Her best hope lay in reaching the main road, where she might get a bus or a taxi the rest of the way. But her walk went on and on with no sign of hope.

The light was fading, and when a hut appeared in the distance ahead of her she could only just make it out. It had started to rain. Just a soft drizzle at first, but it had swiftly become a downpour. She began to run, heading for the hut, hoping to reach it quickly, but she was already soaked when she got there.

Opening the door, she saw that it was shabby. In the poor light she could see little else, but there was at least a bed where she would be able to rest until light broke next morning.

She stripped off her clothes, seizing the small towel she'd brought with her, and drying herself as well as she could. She put on some basic items from her suitcase and lay down.

Gazing into the darkness, she wondered at herself for choosing this way out.

Might she not have stayed in the *castello* with the man who had once seemed to be winning her heart? Did she *really* have no chance of winning his?

Maybe she was being cowardly, running away, but what choice did she have? How could she stay with Vittorio knowing she could never win his love when he was so determined not to let her? No, she'd served her purpose. He'd paid the debt, assuaged his guilt, and now he'd surely be relieved to see her gone. Besides, she was glad to get away from him—wasn't she?

CHAPTER TEN

FOR WHAT FELT like hours Vittorio sat at his desk, trying to concentrate. At last he threw down his pen and faced facts. As so often before, the infuriating woman had wiped everything except herself from his mind.

If they were to have a future together she'd have to learn that he must sometimes think of other things. And the sooner they sorted it out the better.

He went to her bedroom and opened the door.

But she wasn't there.

Downstairs, he searched room after room without finding her. Tearing his hair, he went to the kitchen to find Gina.

'Do you know where Jackie is?' he asked.

'I saw her go out an hour ago.'

'Go out? Where?'

'For a walk, I think. She was carrying a case,

but she couldn't have been going far or she'd have asked Leo to drive her.'

'Did she leave a message?'

'No, Signor Conte.'

So now Gina knew he'd been deserted, and suddenly it was unbearable that she should see him at such a moment.

In fury and despair he ran upstairs to his bedroom. There on the floor he found Jackie's note, and read it with mounting disbelief.

Downstairs he confronted Gina again. 'Which direction did she go?'

'In that direction.' She pointed through the window.

The path she indicated led to the main road and ultimately to Rome. Given the note Jackie had left him, the meaning was obvious.

'Poor Jackie,' Gina said. 'It's raining so hard now. How terrible for her. Shall I tell Leo to go after her?'

'No need,' Vittorio said through gritted teeth. 'I'll go myself.'

The rain seemed to get heavier as he headed for the car. What on earth had possessed her to do this?

The only possible answer appalled him.

She was heading for Rome—perhaps the railway station, perhaps the airport. Whichever it was, she was on her way back to England, leaving him with her cruel message and nothing to hope for.

Through the darkness the car's headlights flooded the road ahead, showing no sign of her. But she *must* be somewhere near here, he thought frantically. In the time she'd had to walk she couldn't have got much further than this.

Then he saw the hut, and pulled up quickly.

There were no lights on inside, but he had a torch in the car and took it with him.

He opened the door tentatively, unable to see much. 'Is anybody there?' he called.

The response was a choking sound. Turning his torch to the far wall, he saw Jackie lying on a bed.

'Jackie!'

He rushed forward and knelt beside the bed.

'What the hell are you doing, leaving like this?' he demanded. 'Are you mad?'

'Yes,' she murmured. 'I had to get away from you.'

'Because I'm a monstrous bully. That's what you called me, and you were right. I'm a bully and I'm about to prove it. I'm taking you home with me. Don't argue. You're coming with me whether you want to or not—because you're soaking wet and I'm not leaving you here to get pneumonia. If you refuse then I'll be forced to carry you.'

'You think I'm just going to give in to your bullying?'

'Why not? When we were in that hotel you bullied *me* to stop me driving home and I gave in, didn't I?'

She rubbed a hand over her eyes. 'Then I guess I can't say no...' She sighed.

'Wise woman.'

He helped her to her feet. At once she swayed, making him seize her urgently.

'I'd better carry you anyway,' he said.

'No, I can manage.'

'Jackie, please—'

'I said I can manage. Let me go. I don't need your help.'

He released her, but stayed close, keeping his hands only a few inches away, so that she could cling to him if necessary. She managed to get to the door without needing him, but then let him support her the last few yards.

She had insisted that she didn't need his help,

but as he eased her into the car she had to admit that she wasn't sorry to be returning to warmth and comfort.

Ten minutes brought them back to the house, where Vittorio parked the car before helping Jackie out.

'Go up to bed,' Vittorio said. 'I'll send Gina to dry you off and make sure you're well.'

It was lovely to snuggle down in the comfortable bed, and even lovelier to reflect on what had just happened. True, Vittorio had shown his authoritative side, insisting that she return. But he'd also shown his kinder side, looking after her carefully as he'd driven home.

It was the same old confusion. Which man *was* he? The coldly authoritative one who would tolerate no disagreement? Or the gentle, concerned one who kept a kind eye on her needs?

He was both, she decided.

There was a tap at the door.

'Can I come in?' he asked.

'Yes, come in.'

'I had to see how you were.'

'I'm very sleepy, but I don't feel too bad.'

'Then you must have a nice long sleep.'

He reached out for the blanket and drew it up over her shoulders. She snuggled down blissfully.

'I'm sorry if I caused you a lot of trouble,' she said. 'It was just—'

'I think I know what it was.' He sat down on the bed. 'When you're better we must have a talk to see if we can sort out all the ways we misunderstand each other. It's strange when you remember how many times we've noticed how well our minds connect. Yet sometimes the connection fails.'

'It comes and goes,' she mused, 'but will we ever really understand each other? We're so different.'

'*Are* we different? Haven't we found a hundred ways in which we're the same?'

'Yes,' she murmured, 'I guess so...'

As she spoke her eyes closed. Vittorio watched as her breathing grew deeper, more peaceful. When he was sure she was asleep he took a gentle hold of her hand.

'It's been a lesson for both of us,' he said. 'And there's still some way to go. But we'll get there, won't we?'

When she didn't reply he leaned down and whispered in her ear.

'We will, because we must. We really must, Jackie.'

He laid his lips softly against her cheek and left the room quickly, before she could wake.

Jackie slept well that night, and the next morning went downstairs to find Vittorio already eating breakfast.

'How are you this morning?' he asked.

'Fine.'

'Good. We must get things sorted out.'

'What things?' she asked cautiously.

'We've got the ball to think about. It wasn't very kind to Tania, the way you dashed off. Hate *me*, if you want to, but don't take it out on her.'

'I don't hate you.'

'Really? You could have fooled me.'

'That was because you'd forced that money on me. You're so sure you can buy me off, aren't you? But you can't. I want you to take it back.'

'No way.'

'If you don't take it back I'll be out of here tomorrow.'

'You'll—? After all we—? Surely we agreed on that?'

'No, you *thought* I'd agreed because I shut up

about it. But I still feel the same. If I accept that money I'll be saying that my father's suffering doesn't matter. But it *does* matter. It matters more than anything in my life. It would be an insult to him that I couldn't endure. Why do you want to make me suffer?'

'The last thing I want is for you to suffer,' he said, speaking the truth.

'Then what are you going to do?'

He picked up the phone, dialled a number and engaged in a sharp-sounding conversation in Italian.

When he'd put the phone down he said, 'I've told the bank that transferring that money to you was a mistake and they're to transfer it back.'

'Will it work? Won't they say that since it's in my account I have to tell them myself?'

'Perhaps they should—but they'll do what I tell them. Let me show you.'

In his office he switched on a computer, logged in to his bank and showed her that the money had immediately been transferred.

He stared at the screen, feeling blank despair at what it told him. He'd promised his father to return the money to Jackie, and felt glad when he'd managed to do so. But now he'd yielded, taken it back, and in his heart he'd betrayed his beloved father.

Jackie was also staring at the screen, trying to take in the incredible sight that she could see.

'They just obeyed you,' she murmured. 'However did you persuade them?'

'I've got a place on the board.'

'Of course. Why didn't I think of that? Is there anywhere you *don't* have power?'

Suddenly his temper rose. 'Are you out of your mind to say that? You just told me what to do and I did it. Who obeyed whom? And you dare to accuse *me* of having all the power.'

'I'm—I'm sorry,' she stammered. 'I didn't think—'

'Do you *ever* think? You've got it so firmly fixed in your mind that I'm a controlling bully that you never look at our relationship closely enough to see how often it's the other way around. You told me to get on to the bank and transfer the money, and I did it straight away!'

'Yes, I'm sorry. I didn't see it that way—'

'No, because it doesn't fit your convenient picture of me. Heaven help me if I do something that doesn't fit your expectations. You'll wipe it out of your mind the way you tried to wipe *me* out.'

'Stop it,' she cried, suddenly weeping. 'Please stop.'

Tears had come without warning. She turned her head but it was too late. He'd already seen them.

'Hey, come on, there's no need for that.' His rage vanished and he took her into his arms, resting her head on his shoulder. 'Don't cry,' he said kindly.

She pulled herself together and drew back.

'You're wrong,' she said huskily. 'I *do* know you can be nice.'

'However hard it is for you to admit it?' he said, smiling.

'I'm sorry.'

'Enough of that. It's good that we're talking. We can sort everything.'

'Can we? There's so much to be sorted.'

'I know. But we can do anything if we try. Come here.'

He drew her close and placed a kiss on her mouth. It was gentle rather than passionate, and it warmed her heart.

'Sit down and have some coffee with me. Then we can plan what we're going to tell Tania.'

'She doesn't know about what happened yesterday?'

'Nothing happened. As far as she's concerned you didn't dash off and banish me into the wilderness.'

'I certainly didn't banish you into the wilderness!'

He regarded her wryly. 'That depends on what you mean by "wilderness".'

He guessed she had no idea of the bleak desert in which he'd found himself when he had found her gone. It had felt like the worst kind of wilderness. And that had alarmed him because clearly there was no wilderness for her.

'We'll have to get to work on the ball,' he said. 'Tania's counting on our help.'

'Yes. You're right. I should have thought of that before I left. I was selfish.'

He touched her face. 'You're not selfish. You just panicked at the thought of being stuck with me for life. We all panic.'

'You? Surely not. I can't believe you *ever* panic.'

Briefly he recalled the wild churning of his stomach when he'd found her goodbye note.

'You're right,' he said quickly. 'Not me. Ever. Now, let's—'

He was interrupted by a beep from the computer.

'It's an email I've been waiting for,' he said.

He did a quick check and opened the new message.

'It's from the store,' he said. 'Some stuff we ordered has started to arrive. I need to be there.'

'I'm coming with you. We'll go to the store and then on to the railway station to meet Tania.'

They drove into town, straight to the store, where they found a mountain of new arrivals. Jackie was briefly nervous, lest they be more of the glass statues that had caused their row, but these were different items. They had come from England and they pleased Vittorio.

'Great,' he said, looking at them. 'Well done, Jackie. I did the right thing promoting you and doubling your salary. You're really benefitting the store.'

She smiled and thanked him, but at the back of her mind was a sense that his action was rooted in their disagreement over money that constantly haunted them. It was always there. When he couldn't give her money one way he found another way to lavish it upon her. Would this nightmare ever go away?

Another thought troubled her. She knew the need to fulfil his father's wishes was so vital to Vittorio that he would seek to keep her close to him until he'd achieved what he sought. Was it anything but that? When he had eased his pain would he feel able to dismiss her?

For another half-hour they worked in his office. Then a knock on the door made him look up to see Donna from the clothes department.

'I've brought what you ordered, Signor Conte.'

Carrying a large parcel, she advanced into the room, laid it on his desk, and departed.

'Have a look,' he said to Jackie. 'It's yours.'

Puzzled, she opened the parcel—and stared at what she found there.

'The dress!' she gasped. 'The one—'

It was the black satin dress she'd tried on when she'd first visited the store.

'It's a gift,' he said.

'You're *giving* this to me? You mean that?'

'You can wear it at the ball.'

'But Tania says I'm supposed to be Lady Nanetta.'

'That's up to you. You *can* be Lady Nanetta—

severe, rigorous, terrifying every man she meets. Or you can be a different woman…the one I saw in this gown the other day.'

'And what is *she* like?'

'I'm not quite sure. I'm still waiting to find out.'

In truth, he felt he already knew. When he'd chanced upon her wearing the seductive gown, its satin clinging to her figure, he had discovered something startling about her and how she could affect him. The time had not yet come when he could speak of it, but the moment *would* come. He promised himself that.

'I'll wear it with the diamond necklace you gave me,' she murmured.

'And you'll be the belle of the ball.' He paused. 'You know, it would help me if we could seem like we're even more of an item. Maybe engaged? And it will help you look the part. I don't want Marisa and the others to think I'm in need of a wife!'

'Okay, I'll do my best,' she agreed simply, knowing if she said much more she would start grilling him about exactly what he was looking for.

And she didn't even know what she wanted

as the answer. Did he want a bride—just not Marisa? Or did he not want a bride *ever*?

'Come now,' he said, interrupting her thoughts. 'Let's take this with us and go to meet Aunt Tania at the station.'

When the train drew in an hour later they were there, waiting for Tania.

'Lovely to see you both,' she declared when they had all embraced. 'How are you getting on? Not strangled each other yet?'

'We're saving that until after the ball.' Jackie chuckled.

'Splendid. Nice to know that you can put important things first. We've got a mass of things to do...'

From the moment the next day dawned it was clear that Tania had been right. The castle was buzzing with preparations.

Over the next few days quantities of extra food were delivered and temporary staff were hired. A television company had even made contact.

At last the great day arrived. In her room, Jackie donned the black satin gown.

'Can I come in?' Vittorio called.

'Yes.'

He entered the room. 'How's this?' he said.

He was wearing the historical costume of the man in the portrait of Lady Nanetta. Jackie stood back to survey him, hardly able to believe her eyes. As had been fashionable at the time, the white trousers were tight-fitting, emphasising the fact that Vittorio's legs were long, slim and attractive.

And sexy, she thought, against her will.

'What do you think?' he asked, turning to give her a better view.

'I think that costume is very…efficient,' she said coolly.

'Yes. Luckily it fits me. And I think *you* chose the right dress. That one will lure every man in the room.'

'*Every* man?' she teased. 'Every single man?'

'Well, you can't ignore me tonight, can you? Not when everyone's expecting to hear that we're engaged.'

'No, I promise to do whatever you want.'

'Do you *know* what I want from you?'

She looked up at him with shining eyes. 'I'm sure you'll let me know.'

'You can count on it. Now, we must make everything perfect. Why aren't you wearing the necklace I gave you?'

'I've tried to put it on but I can't fasten it. It's too difficult.'

'Give it to me.'

He took the necklace and moved behind her, reaching around her neck to position the jewels. She tensed at the feeling of his fingers brushing her flesh.

At last he turned her so that he could look at her face. 'Are you all right?' he asked. 'Nervous?'

'I'm fine.'

From outside they heard the noise growing.

'People are beginning to arrive. Let's take a look.'

Going to her window, they looked out. They could see cars arriving, discharging their passengers. Wide-eyed, Jackie looked at the costumes that were appearing.

Some were obvious fancy dress—clowns, animals—others were historical costumes.

Tania appeared behind them.

'You look very fine,' she told Jackie. 'You'll be a big success. *Oh!*'

The exclamation was drawn from her by the

sight of a splendidly attired couple whose arrival
had caused others to stare in admiration.

'Whoever are *they*?' Jackie asked in astonishment.

'The Duke and Duchess of Revendo. I must go
down and welcome them in.'

Tania vanished, leaving Jackie staring down
at the couple.

So *that* was the woman who had broken Vittorio's heart by dumping him for a loftier man.
She turned her head to look at Vittorio. He was
looking down at the Revendos but his face revealed nothing at all.

It never does, she thought. *Whatever he's feeling, he doesn't want anyone to know. It's almost
as though he's afraid of the world.*

She gave a brief gasp of laughter.

*Afraid of the world. He'd be so mad at me if he
knew I was thinking that.*

But it was true. Vittorio didn't trust anyone.
Even her.

'What's funny?' Vittorio asked sharply.

'Nothing. Why?'

'You laughed. Why? Is the crowd below so
funny?'

'Some of them.'

'Meaning Elena Revendo? I expect Tania's told you about her, hasn't she?'

'Yes,' she said reluctantly. 'But you told me about her first. How can you bear to invite her?'

'Why not? She did me a great favour. Because of her I know things about female deceit, ambition and greed I might not have learned soon enough to be useful. As it is—'

'As it is you learned that lesson in time to distrust every woman you ever meet. Good for you. What would life be like if you made the mistake of *trusting* a woman?'

He regarded her wryly. 'There *is* one woman I trust,' he said. 'One who isn't greedy for money or a title, who's intelligent, honest, and brave enough to express her opinion even when it annoys people.'

The gleam in his eyes made it obvious that he meant her. It might be unwise to feel flattered by such ironic praise, but she couldn't help it.

'You mean when she annoys *you*,' she said. 'Does she annoy anyone else as much as you?'

'I doubt it. Infuriating me is something she's brought to an art form.'

'She sounds like a nightmare,' she observed

lightly. 'For safety's sake you should avoid her like the plague.'

'I try, but she has a habit of popping up in my mind when I'm not expecting her.'

'Then the answer's obvious. Expect her all the time. She's so awkward that it'll make her stay away just to confuse you.'

He grinned. 'Yes, she enjoys confusing me.'

From below, they could hear the orchestra start to play.

'It's time we went down,' he said.

Offering her his arm, he walked with her, out and along the corridor to the top of the stairs.

As soon as they appeared there was a squeal from below. Everyone looked up to enjoy the sight of their elegant entrance. Some of them laughed, some cheered, some applauded.

Jackie had no difficulty seeing Marisa's face. She was at the front, staring up at them with an expression that could not hide her dismay.

Wondering if Vittorio had noticed, she gave him a sideways glance. He returned it, smiling. She smiled back, happy to know they were in this together.

Marisa, watching them from below, scowled.

Most of the guests had heard about Jackie, and

eagerly crowded forward to be introduced to her. It was clear she was the star of the evening, and every guest, male and female alike, seemed to be charmed by her.

Vittorio revelled in the attention Jackie was receiving, but soon enough was enough. He wanted her to himself for a while.

'Shall we dance?' he asked.

Together they proceeded to the ballroom, where the orchestra had just started a waltz.

'We've fooled them,' he said, turning her gently around and around. 'Let's give them a bit more.'

'By doing what?'

'Can't you smile at me as though I'm your heaven on earth?'

'But what would that prove?' she asked. 'Only that I'm one of the crowd chasing you. Now, if *you* smiled at me that would be better. But don't worry. I understand why you don't want to.'

'Don't I?'

'Heaven on earth? *Me?* More like purgatory, driving you mad.'

'Which is just how you like it.'

'I can't deny that.'

They laughed together. Those dancing near them observed them and assumed that they

were in perfect accord and exchanged significant glances.

'Now we've *really* given them something,' she
teased.

'And if they were to hear me tell you that you
look wonderful tonight they'd enjoy that even
more.'

'No, don't say that. Some of them already want
to murder me.'

'But I *want* to say it.' He raised his voice.
'You're lovelier than I've ever seen you.'

'Hush, don't overdo it.'

They laughed again. Then he whirled her
around and around until the music came to an
end.

'That was a great dance,' he said. 'I hope we
can have another one before the night is over.'

'I'm sure we can. But now you have your duty
to do with every hopeful woman here.'

'Yes, ma'am.'

Turning away, she found herself facing Vittorio's Baron friend—the one she had recently
met in the city.

'Stefano,' she said happily. 'How lovely to see
you.'

'And you, *signorina*. I remember our meeting with great pleasure. Since then I've hoped to meet you again. Shall we dance?'

'That would be lovely.'

He put his arm around her waist, drew her close, and began to spin her into the dance.

CHAPTER ELEVEN

STEFANO WAS AN expert dancer, and Jackie found her own moderate skills rising to meet his. It was an exhilarating experience. With his help she discovered her feet could move faster and in more complex movements than she had ever dreamed.

'That was great,' he said as the music ended. 'Now let's waltz together.'

'Yes, let's,' she said, moving into his open arms.

The gentle movements of the waltz made it easier for her to look around at the other dancers. One couple stood out. Vittorio was dancing with the Duchess of Revendo.

'Oh—' she gasped.

'What is it?' Stefano asked. 'Are you feeling unwell?'

'No, I'm fine. Everything's fine.'

'I'm not sure I believe you. When people say it like that things are never really fine.'

'Yes, they are,' she said quickly.

This was something she couldn't bear to talk about. She tried to catch a glimpse of Vittorio's face, to see if it revealed any emotion. But as he whirled around with the woman who had once meant everything to him there was only a blankness in his face that might have meant indifference, or an emotion too strong to reveal.

But then he smiled. And his partner smiled back at him. And suddenly they seemed magically connected.

It lasted only a moment before they turned away, out of Jackie's sight. She took a deep, troubled breath, wondering what life was doing to her and what it would do next.

'You're not going to have any trouble finding partners,' Stefano said as the dance came to an end. 'Look at them all, watching you.'

He was right. There was another offer for her to dance, and then another. She accepted two partners, and then Stefano came forward and claimed her again.

'You're the belle of the ball,' he said as they twirled.

'Only because I'm dancing with the best dancer

in the room!' she said. 'I gather you've got quite a reputation.'

'For dancing?'

'Only partly,' she teased.

She recalled what Vittorio had said about Stefano and his reputation as a playboy.

He was handsome, delightful, and he could make her laugh. Many women would have fallen for him, but these days Jackie was too wise. All sorts of new feelings had grown within her now, protecting her from a man as obvious as this.

But to spend a few minutes dancing with him was an innocent pleasure.

'How are you coping with Vittorio?' he said.

'He's not easy, but I don't manage too badly.'

'Everyone knows he's in love with you and heading for the altar.'

'Nonsense,' she said firmly, remembering Vittorio's face as he'd danced with the Duchess.

'Apparently he told someone at the bank that you were engaged.'

'Oh, that—oh, no. That was just a careless mistake.'

He chuckled. 'Who do you think you're kidding? If there's one man who would never make that kind of mistake it's Vittorio.'

'Yes, but—I'm not one of those women chasing him.'

'Of course you're not. That's why you've caught him.'

'Oh, nonsense. I haven't.' She thought for a moment. *'Have* I?'

'Don't you think you have? Or didn't you want to?'

'I haven't quite decided about that yet.'

A burst of laughter overcame him and Jackie joined in, unable to help herself.

Feeling her shake in his arms, Stefano grasped her more firmly. 'Steady,' he said. 'Don't lose your balance. Hold on to me.'

She did so, and felt herself once more whirled dramatically across the floor,'

Standing near the door with Vittorio, Tania was regarding them with her head on one side.

'The man Jackie's dancing with,' she said. 'Isn't that Stefano?'

'Yes.'

'I hope you warned her about him. Women lose their hearts to him so easily.'

'Not Jackie,' Vittorio observed. 'She never loses her heart to *anyone*.'

'Is that personal experience talking?' asked Tania curiously.

'It could be.'

'But you haven't decided yet? Perhaps you should take your own advice.'

'What advice is that?'

'You once told me that a shrewd businessman never lets a good deal escape him. Seize it while it's going, you said. Perhaps *there's* your deal.'

'A businessman?' he murmured. 'Is that all I am?'

'At one time you'd never have doubted it.'

'At one time I was a different man.'

As they watched the dance ended. At once another man appeared to claim Jackie, who went happily into his arms. The two of them waltzed contentedly until the music ended, at which moment two more young men approached her, both trying to claim her. All around them the other dancers paused to enjoy the sight.

'Don't let a good deal escape,' Tania urged.

'You're right,' he said. 'Time I acted.'

He strode out onto the floor, arriving just as

the two hopeful men were getting deep into argument.

'Sorry to break up the party,' he growled. As he spoke he put his arms around Jackie, drawing her close in a clasp too firm for her to resist. 'But the lady belongs to *me*.'

'Do I?' she asked lightly.

'You do. And if you don't know it now you soon will.'

Vittorio knew a strange feeling as he took her into his arms. Only a few minutes ago she'd been dancing with a well-known charmer, gazing up into his face, collapsing with delighted laughter, and then whirling away with him as though aiming for another world.

Now she was in his own arms, looking coolly up into his eyes and thinking—

Just what *was* she thinking? What lurked behind her gaze?

'I warned you not to fall for Stefano,' he said.

'I didn't. I was just being polite.'

'Polite to him *and* every other man in the room—thus making me look an idiot.'

'Why should it affect you?' she asked lightly.

'Because there's a rumour that we're engaged.'

'A rumour *you* started, for your own convenience. You just wanted to get the better of me about our disagreement.'

'And yet somehow you're the one who always finishes on top,' he observed. 'Isn't that strange?'

'Not strange at all, seeing that I've got right on my side,' she said.

'You *always* think that, don't you?'

'Sure—it's something I learned from you. Oh, boy, the things you've taught me! Get your own way at all costs. Never ask anyone else's opinion, and if they dare to offer one tell them to shut up.'

'I didn't ever tell you to shut up,' he protested.

'Not in words, but you don't need words. Why are you complaining? I had a few dances…enjoyed some innocent fun. It didn't do you any harm. We're not really a couple. We just made a bargain.'

He didn't answer. He had an uneasy feeling that the bargain was slipping away.

'Vittorio, listen to me. You claim that all women are deceitful liars, playing one man off against another. So what are you saying now—that I'm just one of them? Am I no better than the Duchess?'

'Leave her out of this.'

'How can I when you made such a point of dancing with her?'

'That was a courtesy. I danced with her to show that she doesn't trouble me. She did once, but now when we meet things are different.'

'Different? That could mean anything.'

'It means that my heart no longer belongs to her. It belongs to someone else—but I shouldn't have to tell you that. You should know without words.'

'Perhaps,' she whispered. 'But sometimes words can help.'

'Or they can make things worse—which they often do with us. Why are you so determined to quarrel with me, Jackie?'

'*I'm* determined to quarrel?'

'You know how badly I want to sort things out between us. Maybe I was clumsy about the money, but I was desperate to put things right between us, to make you stop hating me because of your father. You can see that, but you won't yield an inch.'

'Why *should* I? Stop this, Vittorio. You talk of putting it right, but nothing will *ever* put it right for my father because he isn't here any longer. If I took the money from you his tragedy would still

be the same as it always was. The only difference would be my conscience, tormenting me because I'd benefitted from his suffering, knowing
that after all his lovely treatment of me I'd just
shrugged my shoulders and said it didn't matter.'

'Would he have blamed you for that?'

'No, he'd have told me to put myself first.'

'Then *listen* to him.'

'I can't take advantage of his sweet nature. I
owe him better. But, Vittorio, this is no time to
venture over such dangerous ground.'

'You could be wrong.' His arms tightened,
drawing her closer. 'Perhaps the best way to tread
on dangerous ground is in each other's arms.'

'Perhaps,' she agreed.

'Sometimes I think "perhaps" is the most troublesome word in the world. *Perhaps* I have feelings for you that frighten me. *Perhaps* you have
the same, but you fight them off.'

'Perhaps...' she said, giving him a challenging look.

They were dancing slowly past a large open
door. Suddenly he whirled her through it and into
a dark corridor.

'What are you *doing*?' she demanded.

'Finding out what "perhaps" means.' His voice

became intense. 'There's something I need to know. Jackie.'

'What?'

'This.'

He dropped his head so that his mouth covered hers. For an instant she tried to resist, remembering their last kiss which had ended in rejection. But the feel of his mouth was thrilling, devastating. Her mind sought to reject him, but her flesh warmed and trembled with pleasure.

Her arms seemed to go about him of their own accord, drawing him closer, seeking something that only he could give her. She moved her lips against his, revelling in the excitement of his response. She had the sudden devastating conviction that he was hers. He belonged to her because that was what he had chosen.

And with shattering conviction she knew that if she weakened she would belong to him. But how weak did she dare to be?

He raised his head a little. Her mouth was free but she could still feel the whisper of his breath against it.

'Well?' she murmured. 'Did you find the answer you wanted?'

'Perhaps…perhaps…' he said softly. 'There was

just a hint. But you're not going to let me guess too soon, are you?'

Her smile teased and challenged him. 'If it's true you shouldn't need to guess. You should *know*.'

'Only if you'll *let* me know. You like to keep me wondering, don't you?'

'It can be fun,' she said.

'There's more in this for us than fun, Jackie. Can't you feel that?'

'I'm not sure *what* I feel. I'm still waiting for you to teach me.'

'Devil! Witch! Stop playing games with me.'

'All right,' she whispered, and drew his head down again until his lips touched hers.

She knew at once that she'd taken him by surprise, and a sudden determined impulse made her embrace him with greater fervour, enveloping him with her desire and rejoicing in his responding passion.

'Vittorio—'

'Jackie— Jackie—'

There was something in his voice that made her heart soar. But suddenly it was all over. He released himself from her and stepped back.

'Why do you torment me, Jackie?'

'I don't—'

'Don't deny it. You knew what you were doing tonight would drive me mad. That's how you get your pleasure, isn't it?'

'I've told you—'

'Did you enjoy dancing with them knowing what the sight of you was doing to me?'

'But I *didn't* know. How was I supposed to know you cared either way? You don't care about me. You pretend to for the sake of our audience, but it's all an act—'

'And *that's* why you hate me? Oh, yes, you've made yourself very plain about that. You hate me because I gained from what my father did to yours. You say all those polite things about how *he* did it, not me. But I see the truth in your eyes every time you look around this place. You see him, don't you? You see your father standing there. And he tells you to hate everything—including me.'

'Yes, he's here for me, but he doesn't tell me to hate. Hatred was never his way. All I feel is his love, which will always be with me.'

Before he could answer there was a shriek of laughter from further along the corridor. Instinctively they both backed off.

'Do you want to go back to the ball?' he asked.

'Not yet—I'm not quite ready.'

'Nor I. Let's stay away together for a while.'

'I'd like to go and have a cup of tea.'

'Tea? Not coffee? Ah, yes, you're English aren't you? Come along.'

Smiling, he offered his arm and they went along the corridor to the kitchen together.

But a surprise was waiting for them. There were already several young women in the kitchen, and as they neared she heard one of them say, 'What a shock Jackie must have given you all!'

The reply came in Italian, causing the first woman to say, 'I don't understand Italian. You know I don't.'

'*Scusami.* In English you would say Signorina Jackie is fooling herself. She thinks she can win Vittorio, but she doesn't know him. Jackie hasn't got a chance, but she's too stupid to realise that. Vittorio will take her to his bed, have what he wants, then throw her out. And *we'll* all have a good laugh.'

Jackie began to shake. To hear all this with Vittorio standing there, hearing it as well, was a nightmare.

'Are you sure he'd do that?' someone asked. 'He might really be in love with her.'

'Get real. Vittorio's *never* really in love with anyone. I've seen the way he looks at her,'

'So have I,' said a voice that sounded like Marisa's.

Jackie tensed as the voice continued.

'And *I've* seen the way he looks at any woman he's trying to seduce. That special expression he can put in his eyes—he's brilliant at that. Fools them every time.'

'I shouldn't think Jackie's easily fooled. I reckon she's tougher than that.'

'That just makes her more of a challenge. It'll make it all the funnier when she realises what a fool he's made of her.'

'But there's a rumour that they're engaged. Apparently he told someone at the bank.'

'I'll bet *he* didn't tell anyone. *She* told someone, trying to back him into a corner.'

'Wasn't he supposed to be engaged to *you*, Marisa? I remember when everyone was talking about it.'

'People talk about everything,' came Marisa's voice. 'What does it matter?'

'Perhaps you should think about Dino Norese,' said someone else. 'He's mad about you.'

'Dino's all right. Nothing special.' Marisa's reply was cool and lofty.

'Let's get out of here fast,' Vittorio murmured in Jackie's ear. 'We don't want them to see us.'

He drew her along the corridor until they were out of danger.

Her head was whirling with what she had heard. The world saw her as a woman foolishly trying to enjoy an impossible conquest and making herself absurd. And Marisa was trying to gain from this too, seeking to reclaim Vittorio.

Some of her words came back to her.

'I've seen the way he looks at any woman he's trying to seduce. That special expression he can put in his eyes...'

That special expression. She had seen that expression in his eyes, and it had pleased her more than she cared to admit.

He wanted her. She wanted him to want her. And there lay danger.

Suddenly Vittorio stopped, taking hold of her shoulders and looking determinedly into her face.

'You're not taking any notice of that nonsense, are you?' he demanded. 'Do you *really* believe

I'm trying to lure you into bed for the pleasure of dumping you afterwards? Is that what you think? *Is it?*'

'No,' she protested. 'But obviously it's what everyone else thinks. It makes me look like the biggest fool on earth. I've got to get out of this place—and this time I'm going to leave for good.'

'Jackie, please think straight. If you leave again you'll make *me* look like the biggest fool on earth.'

'Can't you understand? They think I'm so desperate to marry you that *I* spread the rumour we're engaged.'

'And if I know one thing about you it's that you're *not* desperate to marry me. This is my fault, for what I said at the bank. And I have to put it right.'

'Fine. Go back there and tell them the truth.'

'What truth?' he demanded. 'We have so many truths, and some of them contradict each other.'

'The truth that we fight all the time—that we don't trust each other and can't talk without hurling accusations.'

'That won't convince them that we're not going to marry. Quite the reverse. Some of the most successful couples I know keep up their battle from morning till night. I'm beginning to think we're perfectly suited to each other.'

'Very funny.'

'True—it *is* funny. I like a laugh. The thought of laughing with you for the rest of my life has a certain appeal.'

'But laughter fades after a while,' she said. 'We've got to be sensible.'

'Sensible? Us?'

'Yes, it doesn't sound likely, does it? But I think it's time to put things right.'

'How do you want to do that?'

'We return to the ball separately. We're very polite to each other—'

'You mean with the kind of frigid politeness people use when they actually want to murder each other?'

'Yes. But I've had that temptation often enough to know how to overcome it.'

'Okay, I'll obey your orders. We act indifferent, but I think we should have a polite dance with each other.'

'To confirm the indifference,' she said.

'Right. Let's make a start.'

'You go first.'

He went in ahead of her. Jackie waited several

minutes and then she too returned to the ballroom, going at once to where coffee was being served, and talking politely to the guests she found there.

On the far side of the room she could see Vittorio dancing again, talking cheerfully to his partner. He seemed oblivious to her presence—but that was the polite distance they had promised each other.

'Will you dance with me, *signorina*?'

The man standing before her was a duke. Extending his hand, he led her onto the floor, silently announcing to the world that he had heard the rumour of their engagement and she was accepted in Vittorio's high society.

After him she was claimed again and again. There was no doubt that she was a success.

Across the floor she could just make out Marisa, approaching Vittorio, speaking to him intensely. From her expression she seemed displeased, and clearly his reply did not improve her mood.

So he'd made her understand that she had no hope, Jackie thought. But what had he told her about their imaginary engagement?

Her mind was spinning with everything that

had happened that evening. Between herself and Vittorio things seemed to change from moment to moment, leaving her permanently confused.

And now came the moment for which she had been waiting. Vittorio advanced towards her, hand outstretched, and asked theatrically, 'Will you do me the honour, *signorina*?'

She went into his arms, feeling them close around her as they went spinning across the floor. Even as they whirled she was acutely aware of the curious faces following their every movement.

'They've heard the rumours of our engagement,' he said. 'They're trying to decide how true it is. Time to tell them.'

As the music ended he raised his voice.

'Can I have your attention?'

All around them couples slowed to a halt, staring at him curiously.

'I think you know Jackie,' he said. 'Ever since we came here as a couple everyone has wondered about her. Are we lovers? Are we going to announce our engagement soon? Guess what. We've wondered that ourselves. We have our disagreements—sometimes too often. And we've told ourselves—and each other—that these troubles made it impossible for us to be together.'

Jackie turned wild eyes on him. What was he thinking of, to let strangers into their private lives? This way he would make her look more foolish than ever.

'But there's something more important than troubles,' Vittorio declared, still speaking loudly to the crowd. 'And this is it.'

Before Jackie realised what he was doing he pulled her into his arms and laid his mouth passionately over hers. At first she was too stunned to react, but the feel of his lips caressing hers soon took possession of her mind, her heart and her flesh.

From all about them came cheers and applause. Everyone was delighted.

'It's time we gave them the message finally,' he whispered.

'How do you mean?'

Suddenly his arms released her and he dropped down to one knee.

'Jackie, will you marry me?' he called, loud enough for everyone to hear. 'Will you make me the luckiest man on earth? Will you make me unbelievably happy?'

He looked up at her.

'Do I get an answer?' he said.

'Do you really want one? Aren't you just fooling?'

'No, I'm not fooling. Will you marry me?'

'Then my answer…' she took a deep breath '… is yes.'

The cheers were riotous.

She had the dizzying sensation of having won a triumphant victory for the first time in her life. Plain, dull Cinderella had won Prince Charming.

Well, perhaps Prince Charmless, she thought. But she wasn't complaining.

Tania came forward, arms outstretched to embrace her.

'What a lovely thing to happen!' she declared, loud enough for everyone to hear. 'I'm so glad.'

Everyone got the message that despite her low birth Jackie was being welcomed into the Count's family. It was all settled happily and the ball could continue to the end of the evening.

Together Jackie, Vittorio and Tania bade the guests farewell, and at last the castle was empty.

Tania kissed them both.

'He has made the right choice,' she told Jackie.

'It's so lovely to see that just for once he's got it right.'

'Just for once?' Jackie queried comically. 'Surely he gets things right more often than not?'

'You'll find out about that—but hopefully not too soon. Wait until after the wedding before you discover what a clown he can be. Then it'll be too late for you to escape.'

'Thanks a lot, Aunt.' Vittorio said wryly. 'What would I do without you?'

'You'd have married one of those stupid debutantes. As it is, you've got a woman who'll keep your feet on the ground and make you act sensibly.'

'Hush,' said Jackie urgently. 'He doesn't *want* to act sensibly.'

'That's what I like to hear,' Vittorio said, slipping his arm around Jackie's waist. 'A woman who understands me.' He laughed. 'And now I think I'll go to bed. It's been a heavy day. Jackie—we'll celebrate tomorrow. I'll buy you a ring.'

'Lovely,' she said, smiling.

She doubted if he was really tired. He simply wanted to get away from her to sort out his thoughts. She understood, because it was the same with her.

They left the ballroom together. As they went upstairs she waited for him to say something about that devastating scene, but he was silent.

At her door he said, 'We'll talk tomorrow. We have much to say.'

In her room she stripped off the black satin dress, hanging it up with great care. From now on she would treasure it as a sign of the new Jackie.

But who *was* Jackie now? she wondered.

Suddenly she no longer knew.

Was Jackie the woman whose heart reached out to Vittorio despite her sensible resolutions?

Tonight should have been a delight. He had declared his longing for her before the world.

Yet deep within her there was still the suspicion that he wanted to marry her not for love but to silence the troubles that still disturbed him. He longed to make things right with his father's memory. Other people would have found that strange and incredible, but to Jackie, also intent on keeping her father's memory alive, it made sense.

Suddenly there was a slight sound from outside, followed by a click as the door was opened.

'Can I come in?' Vittorio asked.

'Yes.'

'I thought I should come and apologise,' he said. 'It must have been a shock when I sprang that proposal on you. I just got a bit carried away.'

'It's all right. Don't worry. I'm not actually expecting you to marry me.'

'Everyone else is.'

'Meaning Marisa and the other women? Soon she'll grab herself a husband and we can pretend until then.'

Vittorio gazed at her incredulously. 'I said you were a woman who understands me, and I was more right than even *I* knew.'

'I understand you well enough to know you don't want to get married—so don't worry.'

He gave a brief, wry laugh. 'You're only half right about that. Sometimes I'm not keen on marriage, but sometimes I feel that you're the one person who could tempt me.'

She regarded him with her head on one side. 'Temptation is there to be resisted,' she said. 'Be sensible.'

'According to you, I always resist being sensible. Maybe I'm right. Perhaps it's something we should think of.'

'Think of *marriage*?'

'Unless this is your way of rejecting me. Is your answer no, Jackie?'

'I don't know,' she said slowly. 'Everything is so confused between us. We're often friends, but we hover on the verge of being enemies.'

'I know. But somehow enmity just doesn't work. We always return to being—well—'

'Friends?'

'That too, but friendship is too simple.'

'Don't you feel friendship for me?'

'I feel all sorts of things for you that I don't want to feel. I try to fight them, but they fight me back.'

She nodded. 'I know what you mean.'

'Do you remember that night we spent together in Rome?'

She considered. 'I'm not sure we actually spent it *together*. We were on the same bed, but in different worlds.'

'There were some very close moments. I can remember lying in your arms. I wasn't sure how I got there, but it felt wonderful—warm and safe, and as though the whole world had changed and become kinder.'

His gentle tone revived her memory of waking with him, looking into his face and seeing it vulnerable as it had never seemed before. The sight had touched her heart, arousing a feeling of protectiveness towards him that had never entirely faded.

'Yes,' she murmured. 'The world was different.'

'We can make it different, if that's what we want.'

'If we want it badly enough.'

He stroked her face with tender fingers. 'I know what I want, and how badly I want it. But is it what *you* want?'

'Perhaps,' she whispered.

'Ah, yes—perhaps. The word that we said could decide everything. Perhaps we need to know more.'

He drew her closer, placing his mouth over hers.

He was right. They needed to know more. They needed this.

She moved her mouth against his, telling herself that she was merely seeking information, and what she learned sent shivers of delight through her.

But then she was invaded by a thought that made her draw back.

'What is it?' he asked. 'Am I doing something wrong? Don't you want me?'

'Perhaps...' she said, echoing their significant word.

'Is that your way of keeping me doubtful?'

'No, it's my way of saying I want to be sure if you really want me. Have you forgotten that time when you began to kiss me and then backed off, saying I was too vulnerable? You might be going to do that again.'

He groaned, and dropped his head so that she could no longer see his face.

'Why did you do that, Vittorio? Why did you reject me?'

'I didn't reject you. Believe me, Jackie, I didn't. I *forced* myself to let you go. I wanted you so much that I didn't dare go on any more.'

'But why? What would have happened if you'd gone on?'

'We would have made love, and then you would have known—everything.'

'Would I? Do we ever know what "everything" is?'

'Not really. We think we do, but there's always something—' He gave a sigh. 'I meant everything about *me*—how I feel, the power you have—'

'What power? I don't have *any* power. You could turn your back on me and leave at any minute.'

'Could I?'

'Go on—prove it. Reject me.'

He regarded her for a moment with a curious expression, as though he was trying to be quite certain of how she was manipulating him. At last a knowing smile took over his face.

'You know I can't reject you. You're just demonstrating your control and my weakness.'

'Then prove me wrong. Go on. Toss me aside.'

'If I could, I would. But I can't. You have me. I'm yours. Now you can crow with triumph.'

'I don't think I'll do that,' she said, sliding her hands around his face. 'I think I'd rather enjoy exercising my control.' She smiled. 'Kiss me. That's an order.'

He obeyed at once, touching his lips to hers. She waited for the kiss to grow more forceful, but that didn't happen. The soft touch continued, filling her with a sensation of sweetness that made her want to weep with pleasure.

Then he increased the pressure, and suddenly the kiss was as forceful as she could possibly have desired. She responded joyfully, urging him

on further, and felt his embrace grow more intense as he moved towards the bed and drew her
down beside him.

His hands began to explore her body, pulling
away her clothes. Her heart beat more strongly as
things progressed to their inevitable conclusion.

When it was over peace descended on her as
they lay together.

'Are you all right?' he asked, gazing anxiously
down into her face. 'Did I do wrong?'

'Do you *think* you did?'

He shook his head. 'Having you in my arms
feels more right than anything has ever felt before. Do you mind if I stay?'

'For as long as you like.'

He gave a sigh of pleasure and eased down so
that his head lay on her breast.

She enfolded him with an instinctive protectiveness that overcame her to her own surprise.

Who would ever have thought this man would
need her protection? Yet instinct told her that he
did, for reasons that he himself had never suspected.

'Go to sleep, my love,' she whispered. 'I'm
here. I'll always be here for you, as long as you
need me.'

He didn't move, but she felt his breathing grow deeper.

'And you *do* need me,' she murmured.

He slept almost motionless for the rest of the night, and awoke looking lively.

'That was a great night's sleep.' he said. 'No bad dreams. What about you? Did I keep you awake, lying on you in that position?'

'Not at all,' she said cheerfully.

In truth she was feeling slightly stiff, but the pleasure of giving him a peaceful night was stronger than anything else.

'I'd better go before anyone sees me here,' he said, rising quickly.

At the door he turned to look at her anxiously.

'Jackie, things *are* all right between us, aren't they?'

'Perhaps,' she said.

'Perhaps?' He laughed. 'You know, that's a perfect answer. Bye, now. See you later.'

He vanished, closing the door behind him. Jackie lay back, closing her eyes, relishing memories of the night before, wondering where they would lead.

CHAPTER TWELVE

SHE WENT BACK to sleep and overslept, and was late going downstairs. Vittorio wasn't there, and only arrived half an hour later. From the frown on his face it was clear that he was displeased.

'I need a word with you,' he said.

'Has something happened?'

'Yes. I've been in touch with the bank. I wanted to return your money, but I can't. It seems you've put a block on your account so that nothing can be put in it. Did you do that?'

'Yes.'

'Why?'

'Why did *you* try to put the money in again, against my will? You *know* how I feel about it, yet you've tried to force it on me again.'

'So you fought back by blocking your account against me?' he snapped.

'I didn't fight—'

'Didn't you? Isn't that we do?'

'Only when there's no choice!' she cried. 'Why did you try to make me accept that money again?'

'Because it's the right thing to do.'

'The right thing? To ignore my feelings and make me accept something that hurts me? That's the *right thing* to do?'

'I didn't mean to hurt you—'

'No, you just don't care whether you hurt me or not.'

'I'd hoped to help you understand that you're making a fuss about something that doesn't matter.'

'My feelings don't *matter*? Thanks. I was beginning to understand that anyway.'

'Jackie, please talk sense. Why has this issue of money become so important to us?'

'It's not the money itself. It's what it *means*. You want me to take it for your father's sake, and to comfort you, but it wouldn't comfort *me*. The pain would stay with me. And if you had any feeling for me you would understand that. But you don't, and if we stayed together this would be with us all our lives, spoiling everything we might have had. I love you, but I'm beginning to think I could never be happy with you, and I could never make you happy.'

'How can you *say* that? How would you know what makes me happy?'

'Look ahead down the years, Vittorio. Can you really see happiness when we feel so differently about the things that matter?'

'We can make it happen. We don't have to give in just because we have a disagreement.'

'This isn't just a disagreement. It's more important than that. It's a difference that could last all our lives, poisoning everything. It was only because of a disaster that we met in the first place. Perhaps we were never meant to.'

'Stop it!' he said savagely. 'Don't talk like that. *Stop it.*'

'Yes. There's no point in talking, is there?' she said.

She fled the room, desperate to get away from a conversation that was breaking her heart. Against all likelihood Vittorio had claimed her love. Now, before her loomed a vision of a future without him.

He still didn't understand. He thought it was about money, but it wasn't. How could they ever be united as one when they saw life so differently?

In her own room she switched on her laptop,

seeking the distraction it could sometimes give. She forced herself to concentrate on the emotion-less screen, hoping to control all feeling before she yielded helplessly.

An email had arrived. Opening it, she read it.

Things are chaos at the shop without you. Rik has managed to sell it and the new owner is desper-ate for staff who understands the place. Gary.

This was it. The sign she'd been waiting for—her chance to put the past behind her. Vittorio, Rome—everything she wanted to forget.

It had to happen. They weren't right together. She'd thought she could make it work because she loved him, but maybe sometimes love wasn't enough.

Going downstairs, she found Vittorio, as she'd expected, in his office, buried in paperwork.

'I have something to tell you,' she said. 'I'm going back to England.'

'Will you be away long?'

'I'll be away for ever. I'm saying goodbye, Vit-torio.'

'Goodbye? So you really think we no longer have a chance?'

'Did we ever have a chance? We thought we'd got things right at last, but it was an illusion. Let's be honest. We need to forget that we met— and especially forget *how* we met. That has always been a kind of poison between us. Now it's time for us to face the truth and part. And you need never worry that I'll start any legal action. I promise I never will.'

'Is that what you imagine has been troubling me all this time?' he demanded angrily.

'I don't know *what's* been troubling you. I don't think I'll ever understand you any more than you will understand me. It's best that we say good-bye now.'

He gave a bitter laugh. 'Perhaps I should have expected this. You've meant more to me than any other woman because the others were after my title and my money. I valued you because I thought you wanted only me. But you don't want me. So you're right. Let's call it a day.'

His words were like a blow to her heart. If he had said he loved her everything would have changed. But he wanted her only for reasons of pride.

'Yes, let's,' she said. 'I'll call the airport now.'

'Let me do it for you.'

He immediately got on the phone.

After making a few notes he said, 'There's a flight at midday tomorrow. I'll book you on it.'

A few minutes were enough to do the job. Then all was settled.

'I'll print your ticket off for you,' Vittorio said. 'And I'll arrange a taxi to get you there in good time.'

'Will you see me off?'

'Yes, I'll come to the airport and make sure you get on the right plane. We don't want you to get lost, do we? Don't worry. Everything will go well.'

But nothing was going well, she thought sadly. They were parting, and all he cared about was arranging things properly. His insistence that she'd meant more to him than any other woman had been just empty words. She meant nothing to him.

But as she lay in bed that night she managed to find a little hope. There had been times when he'd treated her with something that might have been affection. Perhaps when they were at the airport tomorrow he might show some feeling. Perhaps he'd ask her to change her mind and come back. She would kiss him goodbye and then—*oh, please*—let him kiss her back. Let him discover that they really loved each other. Surely she could make him want her?

Still clinging to hope, she finally fell asleep.

She awoke early, dressed quickly and hurried downstairs, full of hope and determination. She would not give in. Today she would open her heart to Vittorio and persuade him to open his heart to her. It would be a day of victory.

She was smiling as she went into the kitchen.

But there a shock awaited her. There was no sign of Vittorio.

Tania was sitting alone at the table. She looked up and smiled at Jackie.

'Have a good breakfast,' she said. 'Vittorio said you'd be leaving early for the airport. He asked me to tell you goodbye for him.'

'He—what?'

'He got called away to an important meeting. He says he's sorry, but he couldn't help it.'

Jackie drew a sharp breath, fighting back the desire to cry out.

It was over.

He had abandoned her without a word of goodbye, and in doing so he'd made plain his indifference to her.

'I'll leave at once,' she said. 'Goodbye.'

'Must you go?' Tania asked. 'I've so liked having you here.'

'Thank you, but the sooner I go the better. I've turned into a different person here—one I'd better get rid of.'

'But why? It's true you've become another person, but she's very attractive. She's bright and witty, always ready to join in the fun.' Tania smiled fondly, adding, 'She's a true Roman.'

'That's very kind, but my *other* self is actually rather stupid. She's easily taken in because she believes what she wants to believe. Now it's time for her to face facts.'

'But does she know which are the right facts to face?' Tania asked, regarding her curiously. 'Sometimes one makes mistakes about these things.'

'Not this time,' Jackie said with a sigh. 'I got it wrong at first, but now I've seen the light and— well, that's all that matters.'

'But there might still be things you should know.'

Jackie managed a smile. 'If there are, I think I'll discover them at the right moment. Now, I must go and finish my packing.'

She made a quick escape. Tania's unease told its own story. Vittorio's aunt knew that he was up to something that would hurt Jackie badly, and she was unsure what to reveal.

But Tania didn't need to tell her, Jackie thought. Vittorio was angry with her for daring to leave him.

Jackie hurried upstairs. The sooner she was out of here the better.

Tania waited until she was out of earshot, then picked up the phone and dialled a number.

'Vittorio? Is that you? Oh, good. Listen—she's just been down here. I told her that you'd been called away early—no, I didn't tell here where you've really gone. I kept quiet about that, as we agreed. My dear boy, are you sure you're going about this the right way? I know she's an attractive young woman, but she can also be very difficult— All right, I suppose you're right to take the chance, but you might have to duck for safety when she finds out what you've actually been up to today.'

The flight to London seemed to take for ever. Jackie tried to tell herself that one stage in her life was finished and she must prepare for the next. But no common sense thoughts could heal the pain in her heart.

Her love was over—which meant that her life was effectively over. And she didn't know how she would endure it.

Arriving in London, she headed straight for the shop. It seemed strange when she arrived—more restricted, less interesting.

Perhaps she could find a job here. The place apparently needed her.

Going inside, she saw nobody—until a man appeared from the back.

'Can I help you?'

'I'm looking for a job,' she said. 'Are you short-staffed? Do you need anyone?'

He shook his head.

'I'm afraid I can't give you a job. Only the owner can do that.'

'Then can I talk to the owner?'

'I'll fetch him.'

He went deep into the back of the shop and she heard him call, 'Can you come here, sir?'

After a moment a man appeared, the sight of whom made Jackie gasp.

'Vittorio!'

Smiling, he came towards her and laid his hands gently on her shoulders.

'But what are you—?' she gasped. 'How did you get here?'

'I booked you on the midday flight, but I booked myself on the flight at six in the morning. That's why I'd already gone when you woke up. I needed to get here well ahead of you.'

'So *you're* the new owner?' she said, stunned.

'No. You'll find the owner's name here.'

He drew out a piece of paper bearing the owner's name, and showed it to her.

'But that—it's *my* name there.'

'That's because you're the owner,' he said simply. 'Just as your father would have wanted.'

'But Rik—'

'I contacted Rik from Italy and persuaded him to sell to me. A lawyer here finished the formalities, and when I arrived I went straight to the lawyer and transferred the property to you. That's why I needed to get here well ahead of you.'

'But—how am I going to run this place? Are you telling me that it's all right for me to move back to London?'

'No, I'm telling you that you're coming home with me, because I'm not letting you go—now or ever. I hope you agree to that, or I'll be forced to bring my bullying side to the surface.'

There was a gleam of humour in his eyes, but also something else that might have been an anxious plea.

She gave him a warm smile, saying, 'Perhaps you should beware. I might have to bring my bullying side to the surface.'

'And we both know I don't cope with that very well. But it's lucky you're a great businesswoman, because you can organise this place while living with me in Rome. Please, Jackie. *Please.*'

She touched his face. 'I guess it would be heartless of me to refuse. We'll do it your way.'

He smiled and kissed her hand.

'I've taken over the apartment upstairs, where you used to live. Come up with me. I've got something to show you.'

It felt strange to be climbing the stairs to her old home—like moving back in time. Inside she found it much the same as she remembered: plain and basic.

While he made her a cup of tea she studied the papers that made her the owner of the shop.

'However did you do this? And how can I accept it?'

'You can because I've got something else for you—something that will solve the great problem that has always come between us. I mean the money. We will never be at peace over that until we find a final decision that feels good to us both.'

'But is there such a thing? How could there be?'

'I think I've found it. Look at this.'

He handed her a letter that she read with mounting astonishment. It came from a charity and was addressed to her father.

'It says he's donated a quarter of a million pounds,' she gasped. 'But how could he?'

'Easily—with a little help.' Vittorio handed her several more letters. 'Look at these.'

The letters were from three more of her father's favourite charities, each one thanking him for the gift of a quarter of a million pounds.

'*You* did this?' she breathed.

'Let's say I was your father's messenger boy. I told you I'd find a way of handing over the money in a manner that you couldn't resist, and I've done it. It's really just a way of forcing you to do what I want, selfish bully that I am. You said I couldn't understand why this was so important to you, and at first you were right. But then I started to fall for you and the more I came to love you the more I saw it through your eyes.'

'You can *do* that?' she cried joyfully. 'You really understand now?'

'I knew you didn't want the money yourself, but it was painful to you to know that I had it. You told me that we needed a way to return it to him without involving you, but that didn't seem possible.'

'You found one,' she breathed. 'You found it. Look what it says about him.'

She read from one of the letters. '"After his magnificent gift George Benton will be celebrated as one of our greatest benefactors—a man whose generosity knew no bounds and for whom no admiration and respect would be enough."' She looked quickly through the other letters. 'All four of them say something like that. Look!'

He took the papers from her, gazing with a pleasure that matched her own.

'They do him justice,' he said. 'That's the best we could hope for.'

We. The joyful word echoed through her brain. They were together in this.

'We,' she breathed. 'You said "we".'

'It's "we" because now everything matters the

same to both of us. We're a team, and we always will be. Forgive me, my darling, for taking so long to see the light, but now I have seen it. I was desperate for a way to reach out to you and prove that my heart understood yours. I knew nothing else would ever make you love me.'

'And you're right,' she breathed. 'I thought you'd never understand the truth about what was keeping us apart, but you do. And now you've actually found a way—' She seized the letters. 'This is brilliant. I've never been so happy in my life.'

'Then why are you crying?' he asked anxiously, for tears had begun to pour down her cheeks.

'I can't help it,' she wept. 'Suddenly—'

Suddenly she was invaded by an emotion more powerful than any she had ever known.

Vittorio put his arms around her. 'Hold on to me,' he said. 'You're safe now. I'll never let you go.'

'Never? Promise me?'

'I promise. What greater tribute could I pay to your late father than by promising to love, protect and care for his daughter for the rest of her life?'

He kissed her. She returned the kiss joyfully,

then rested against him, feeling the warmth and
sweetness of knowing he was hers for ever.

'Did you always mean to give me the shop?'

'Of course. A man should give his bride a wedding gift. And this is mine to you.'

'A wedding gift?'

'We're getting married. You promised to marry
me ages ago and I'm holding you to that promise. I won't take no for an answer. Say yes. Say
you'll marry me and accept the shop.'

The words sounded forceful, but he said them
with a gentle smile that ended all her fears. Now
she could only do what her heart urged.

'All right,' she said softly. 'I'll marry you. *And*
I'll accept the shop.'

Now that they understood each other perfectly
she could sense that everything was different.
They had reached their destination at last and
there was no more to fear.

They spent the night together—not making
love, but lying peacefully in each other's arms.

In the darkness of the night Jackie awoke to
find Vittorio standing at the open window, looking up into the sky.

She went to stand beside him. 'I think our fathers would be overjoyed that we've found each other. They'd be even more delighted that we've finally begun to love and understand each other in the way they always wanted.'

He put an arm around her. With the other he reached up to the heavens. She followed his gaze to where the stars glittered and the moon glowed.

'They're up there too,' he said. 'Can't you tell?'

'Yes,' she breathed. 'And I think—I think they're shaking hands to congratulate each other.'

'That's what I think too,' Vittorio said.

Then he drew her closer, enfolding her in an embrace that would protect them all their lives.

* * * * *

If you enjoyed this story, check out these other great reads from Lucy Gordon

EXPECTING THE FELLANI HEIR
REUNITED WITH HER ITALIAN EX
NOT JUST A CONVENIENT MARRIAGE
THE FINAL FALCON SAYS I DO

All available now!

Psst!

SAME GREAT STORIES...
STYLISH NEW LOOK!

We're having a makeover!
From next month we'll still be bringing
you the very best romance from authors
you love, with a fabulous new look.

LOOK OUT FOR OUR STYLISH NEW LOGO, TOO

MILLS & BOON

LET'S TALK

Romance

For exclusive extracts, competitions and special offers, find us online:

 facebook.com/millsandboon

@millsandboonuk

@millsandboon

Or get in touch on 0844 844 1351*

For all the latest titles coming soon, visit millsandboon.co.uk/nextmonth

*Calls cost 7p per minute plus your phone company's price per minute access charge